THE FORTRESS OF TIME

A Time Travel romance

Called by a Viking
Book One

Mariah Stone

JOIN THE ROMANCE TIME-TRAVELERS' CLUB!

Join the mailing list on mariahstone.com to receive exclusive bonuses, author insights, release announcements, giveaways and the insider scoop of books on sale—and more!

Upcoming books in the series:

One Night with a Viking

The Jewel of Time

The Marriage of Time

The Surf of Time

The Tree of Time

PROLOGUE

 örnen, Norway, 870 AD

SIGURD'S HEART sank as nine dragon ships appeared from behind a mountain by the fjord. He stood alongside his father, Jarl Randver, on the beach by their village. Ten dozen of their best warriors waited for the enemy right by their side, axes, shields, swords, and bows ready for battle.

The red and blue of the ships' sails screamed the arrival of the enemy, Jarl Fuldarr. It meant that Sigurd's sister, Vigdis, had failed in her mission to negotiate peace and that she was either dead or captured as a hostage, and probably somewhere on board one of those ships.

Sigurd's heart turned into ice at the thought.

It also meant that his men could not send a shower of arrows down on the ships because they were afraid to hurt her.

They waited to find out what Fuldarr had to say.

"It's my fault," Sigurd said to his father, who gripped his

great long ax so hard his knuckles whitened. "I should not have sent her, I should have gone myself."

"It *is* your fault, Son. How many times did I tell you, you cannot trust important things to women." His father gestured at the ships with his ax. "Look at the consequences."

"She begged me to give her responsibility. And she always gets what she wants."

Randver grunted as a shadow of pain passed across his face. He had been sick for a year now, an unknown illness eating him from the inside, pain stealing his sleep and draining his body. Sigurd had been filling his father's role of jarl. He had started building a fortress around the village in anticipation of attacks. The jarldom grew weak; many strong warriors left them because Sigurd could not go raiding. Sigurd had needed to negotiate peace with Fuldarr as they were in no position to withstand such attacks. Sending Vigdis had sounded like a good idea. Yes, she was a woman, but she was a jarl's daughter and proud to have been entrusted with a man's task.

"I should have been stricter with her," Randver said. "She wouldn't have assumed that the world owes her everything. She should have just fulfilled her duties like her mother and like every woman. You should not have trusted her." He turned to Sigurd. "Never trust a woman, Son."

The words reminded Sigurd of his mother and made his muscles ache like the chills before a fever.

What had happened to Vigdis was his fault. Guilt hung in his chest like a rock. He hoped that he had not sent his sister to her death. If Fuldarr had touched a hair on her head, Sigurd would cut out his heart and feed it to pigs.

The ships arrived. Dozens of Fuldarr's warriors scowled at them, but no one moved. On the biggest ship, Sigurd saw Jarl Fuldarr in the richest brynja he had ever seen, his long beard braided, his dark hair combed and oiled, a sable fur cloak falling from his shoulders—it must have shielded him from cold nights on the ship.

Fuldarr watched them without movement. Sigurd gripped the handle of his battle ax, ready to charge or build a shieldwall at his father's command.

A movement caught Sigurd's eye, and a woman's figure appeared next to Fuldarr. Sigurd blinked.

It was Vigdis, alive and whole, her back straight, her long golden hair hidden under a silk scarf—the sign that she was married. Her face was cold like a queen's. She wore the most beautiful dress he had ever seen, the color of a warm summer's sunset, and jewelry of such beauty he had only seen once in a raid on Frankia hung from her neck. A sable fur trim cuddled her throat. It made her look beautiful, just like their mother. The pain of loss hacked at Sigurd's heart at the memory of the first woman who had brought betrayal to their family. His father was right, as usual.

"Are you unharmed, Vigdis?" Randver's voice cut through the air.

Her face lost its proud expression for a moment, and guilt flickered across it.

"I am all right, Father."

"Then, I see, your negotiations went well," Randver said. "I had never wanted you to marry our enemy."

"Fuldarr offered me something you would never do." She raised her chin. "Equal word at his long table. Forever. He's treating me like a queen. Nothing like you treated my mother. Or me."

Randver spat on the pebble beach without breaking eye contact with Fuldarr. "What did you come for, Fuldarr? We are family now, aren't we?"

Silence fell on the beach. Randver whispered under his breath so that only Sigurd would hear. "She told him about

3

all our defenses. That is why he married her. You know what to do. Go."

"I came to claim what's mine!" Fuldarr roared.

Sigurd hissed, "I am not leaving you here. There are twice as many of them."

Randver chuckled, and his bright-blue eyes shone for the first time in a long time. "Son, I will be grateful for this death. A weapon will take my life and not the sickness that has gripped me by the balls like a little boy. Odin will welcome me today in Valhöll, and I will drink mead with him and my father. I will wait for you there when your time comes. Don't hurry though."

He gripped Sigurd's shoulder and squeezed it. "Now, go. Protect the village."

Sigurd's throat clenched. His sister's betrayal, the enemy at their feet, his father's sure death, made bile rise in his throat. The last thing he wanted was to leave his father and his best warriors in the first row of defenses, but he knew Randver was right. The village would need Sigurd to lead their warriors when the first line fell.

"I'll see you in Valhöll, Father." Sigurd squeezed his father's mighty shoulder, and they nodded to each other, their eyes locking for the last time.

He left the row of warriors as they began moving under his father's last cry: "Shieldwall!".

He couldn't believe his sister had betrayed him after the way he'd protected her all her life. His father's words carved traces on his heart: *Never trust a woman, Son.*

As he ran towards the village, arrows began hitting the ground around him like raindrops. Sigurd touched the Thor's hammer pendant that always brought him luck, and whispered, "I won't, Father, I promise."

4

CHAPTER ONE

*N*ew York City, 2018

DONNA COX HAD to win the case, or four clients would not be able to buy bread next month. They waited for the hearing in a court waiting room. Marta and Helena sat to her right, ripe like watermelons. To Donna's left, Teresa and Gloria, both single mothers, whispered in Spanish while rocking two strollers that looked like their best days were long behind.

All four women had been cleaners in a big company, Cinderellas Inc. Their supervisor had fired them as soon as he'd found out they were pregnant. Donna was glad they were brave enough to sue. Most women in their situation did not dare.

Donna's phone rang, and the word "Mom" lit up the screen. Mother was Donna's partner in their two-woman law firm in Brooklyn. Donna held up her index finger to her clients to signal that she'd be right back and went out into the hall.

"Mom? I can't talk. I'm about to go in for the hearing."

"That's why I'm calling. There's been a change, and I'll need you to keep your cool."

"A change?"

"Yes. I found out a minute ago. Ferguson and Partners replaced Virginia with—darn it—with Daniel Gleason."

Heat spread over Donna's cheeks. Daniel Gleason represented everything she passionately despised in the world and the reason she specialized in discrimination lawsuits.

New York swarmed with Daniel Gleasons, and they enjoyed way too much power over women. They ran law firms, hedge funds, and insurance companies. Sometimes, they taught at schools, drove cabs, and mixed cocktails. And one of them had broken Donna's heart.

Daniel looked like a Norse god in a suit. A typical alpha male, he thought only pretty women should be secretaries and that all female CEOs and politicians were lesbians. Three years ago, he had insisted that Donna should stop working, find a rich husband, and give birth to five sons. Back then she had secretly hoped he wanted to be that husband. Despite herself, she had considered following his suggestion because she was in love.

Thank heavens she hadn't. Not that he'd ever proposed. In retrospect, she was glad he'd stopped sleeping with her one day. He'd taught her a lesson.

The lesson she'd thought was part of her DNA, something her single mother had fed her every day with breakfast. To never—*ever*—fall in love with a mouthwatering hunk with a big ego and a sexy smile.

That was why she only dated geeks—often writers or web designers. Guys who respected women. So what if the sex was as stale as day-old champagne. They were smart and funny. They begged her for another date, not the other way around.

"Donna? Are you there?"

Donna blinked, her hand shook. "Yes, Mom."

"Honey. Listen to me. This is the most important lawsuit of your career. Our career. This could be huge for our firm. Put aside your anger. Are you sure you can manage?"

Donna let out a long breath. It didn't help. "I bet this is precisely why they put him on the case."

Mom sighed. "They know the type of men we fight against. Still. You can do it."

"All right. I'm going back in."

"Good luck."

Donna hung up and shook her hands to relieve the pressure. When she went back into the waiting room, an older woman was in her seat. She looked like a universal grandma in small, round spectacles. She knit a wide scarf with a pattern of interwoven tree branches—it reminded Donna of Celtic or Viking art. A golden spindle lay on her lap. Donna did not have time to think about how peculiar she was, because right next to the woman, on Marta's seat, was Daniel.

Donna froze as if she'd hit a glass wall. She had not seen him for three years, and he looked even yummier—and more arrogant—than before. Tall, broad-shouldered, and perfectly built, he sat with his long legs stretched out and ankles crossed. He watched her with a patronizing smirk as if she was a cute little kitten about to fight a bull.

Donna's cheeks flushed from the embarrassment of the unresolved past, and hate burned her like acid. He was using her past feelings against her by being here.

She frowned. Something was wrong in this picture.

Her eight-month pregnant client was standing, rubbing her lower back, leaning against the wall and grimacing in pain, while this son of a butterfly sat on her chair as if he were waiting for a massage in a Turkish sauna.

No. This had not just happened! Fury lit her blood on fire. Donna marched towards them, her heels clacking murder against the marble floor of the courthouse.

"What do you think you are doing, Daniel? You self-centered orangutan! Did you take a pregnant woman's seat? Did you tell her to go back to Mexico? Do you realize we can sue you personally for this? We have witnesses." She pointed at the old lady.

Daniel's face lost all color, and the smirk dropped down his face like a wet towel.

He jumped to his feet. "Donna— No, I'd never— I didn't—"

This was new. She had never seen him stutter like this. Maybe she should throw accusations at him more often.

Marta glanced sheepishly at her. "Donna, as much as I enjoy the show, Mr. Gleason did not steal my seat. My lower back is killing me. I needed to walk."

Mortification struck Donna like a wet snowball. Daniel crossed his arms over his chest, the arrogant smirk lighting up his face again.

"Who will sue now, Donna? But, I feel generous. I'm willing to forget your insults if I can buy you a drink after I win today. Would be great to catch up."

Donna took a deep breath. She realized Daniel had gotten what he'd come for. He shook her off balance, made her emotional, and showed her who was in control.

No, she wouldn't give him the satisfaction. She was a great lawyer. A Harvard graduate. She needed to show him his place. If only she could find the confidence. Everyone was looking at Donna—even the old lady, a sly little smile spreading her lips.

"You know what, Daniel. I will never let you win. You can shove your drink up your nose."

She knew she sounded ridiculous, but anger and embarrassment choked her throat. Why could she not do trash talk?

Donna turned her back to Daniel and, pretending to look through the lawsuit documents, went out of the waiting room into the hall like a high school girl. Thankfully, the hallway was empty, so she could take a breath for a moment.

"Excuse me—Donna, is it?"

Donna turned around, her cheeks still on fire. The old lady with the knitting stood behind her.

"Yes?" Donna took a step towards her.

The woman studied her with the curiosity of a scientist. She had an accent Donna couldn't place. "I could not help but overhear. It seems you have an issue with strong men."

Donna frowned. "I do not have an issue with strong men!"

"Oh, you do, dear. I need you somewhere. No, wrong. There is a man who needs you."

"Needs me? As a lawyer? I mostly represent women against men, so—"

The lady smiled. "Exactly. Could you hold this for me please?"

She held out the spindle, which Donna now noticed was carved tree branches, snakes, and leaves, knotted together in an unending pattern. Donna wondered distantly, who would use a spindle nowadays? Her palm closed around it.

The metal burned her fingertips like a hot cup of tea after a cold day, smooth and sharp. The waiting room disappeared. It was as if something sucked Donna's blood out of her body, a thousand of axes cut her flesh, and a furnace melted her bones. She screamed in pain but only heard the chanting of a man, and she spun and spun like the golden spindle.

And then there was nothing.

CHAPTER TWO

 örnen, Norway, 871 AD

THE MUSCLES of Sigurd's back and arms screamed. His body strained, his fists wrapped around a rope, levering a stake that would become part of the fortress. Made from a giant ancient pine, it was twice as tall as Sigurd. The bottom was planted in a deep ditch.

Sigurd had only one helper—Floki—who was pushing the stake from the other side so that it would stand vertically. They needed at least one more man behind Sigurd to haul the rope and one more to help Floki.

They were building the palisade wall under a massive stone arch that the gods must have carved when they were creating the world. It looked like rocks of different sizes had been stuck together by an invisible force in a rough line between the granite walls of the mountain, forming a natural gate over the dirt path that led to the village.

The palisade wall beneath the arch would protect the

village as part of the fortification system from the west. From the north, the village was shielded by the mountains, but it was vulnerable to overland attacks from the east. The southern side needed the most defense, as it bordered the beach where any raiders coming by sea would arrive.

The mud sucked at Sigurd's shoes, making it hard to get a foothold. So far, the stake was winning.

"Hold!" yelled Floki, his face red, the veins on his neck bulging.

It had been hard labor to build the fortress. Last year's late-summer battle against Fuldarr had taken half of the male population. Sigurd hoped that his father feasted with Odin in Valhöll, for he had fallen in the battle like a hero, taking many enemies with him. Thankfully, Sigurd had won, his second line of defenses tipping the balance to their side. Fuldarr had retreated with only a third of his ships—and with Vigdis.

Fuldarr would not recover soon from such defeat, but neither would Vörnen. The battle, which had lasted many hours, had left them an easy target for raiders. It had been the end of raiding season, thank the gods, so no one had attacked them since. Now it was June, and most neighbors were busy planting this year's vegetables, rye, and barley— too early for raiders yet. They had to finish the fortress as soon as possible, and most certainly before the end of summer, or they'd be an easy target for common raiders. Of even greater concern was next year, by which time Fuldarr would have most likely gathered new troops.

The rope burned Sigurd's hand and creaked softly. He had to pull it up now, or the stake would fall on Floki. If only Sigurd had more men.

He filled his lungs with air and roared "Noooow!" pulling the rope towards him, hoping that Floki would push at the same time.

Asa, Floki's wife, appeared on the path with their lunch in a basket. Her eyes widened and she rushed towards them, basket dropped on the ground. She took the rope behind Sigurd and hauled with him. Sigurd felt that the rope gave easier and the stake started moving towards them, but he grunted. "What are you doing, woman? Go away."

She only groaned and pulled harder. The tip of the log rose up, but too quickly. How was she so strong?

"Go away, Asa!" Alarm rang in Sigurd's voice. She'd surely make a mistake, she had no idea how to do this and was going to get them both killed.

"You need help, jarl," she grunted through her teeth.

Anger rose in Sigurd's stomach like hot bile. He'd seen the kind of help women provided... "I forbade women to come near the fortress!"

Rage gave Sigurd strength he did not know he had. He yanked the rope, and the stake jerked up. It stood vertically for a moment, then lost its balance and fell on the left wall with a thump. The arch above the path cracked in the thinnest place from the blow. Sand and small stones showered on the path below.

Floki jumped away. But the arch did not break.

"Silly woman!" Sigurd growled. "How are we going to build the wall when stones can fall on us at any moment?"

Sigurd caught a movement, and his eyes darted to the ground by the ditch.

A woman lay there.

The air shifted as if heat radiated from the ground, but then it was gone. Freyja, the goddess of love, sprawled on the path, her famous golden hair spilling over the ground around her.

He blinked. How did she get there?

The stake began sliding towards the ground. The friction of the heavy log against the wall shifted the fragile balance of the cracked arch, and a rock the size of a child's head began falling towards the woman.

It all took just a moment, but Sigurd saw it as if time had slowed.

He darted towards the unconscious body and yanked her just enough. The stone hit the ground right where her head had lain.

Everyone held their breath.

Sigurd stared at her. She was the prettiest woman he had ever seen. Her skin was flawless, her eyelids sparkled with hues of golden stardust, her soft pink lips swelled as if calling for a kiss. She wore the strangest clothes he had ever seen: a gray jacket hugged her waist and arms so that she had little room for movement; a skirt clung to her hips and ended just above the knees, shamelessly exposing beautiful legs. Sharp sticks that could pierce a man's eye were glued to the heels of her shiny shoes. Did she use them as weapons?

On her neck lay a golden thread of a necklace of such delicacy that it could only have been crafted with magic by dwarfs from legends. Pearls stuck from her earlobes. An armring around her wrist had one white circle, tiny runes along the edge, and two arrows that pointed at them from the center as thin as bone needles. The armring ticked and one of the arrows moved.

Human hands had not made these objects. "She must be a goddess," Sigurd whispered.

Asa came close. "Is she alive?"

Sigurd pressed his ear against her jacket, warm from the heat of her body. He heard a good *thump-thump*, *thump-thump*. He nodded to Asa. He looked the woman over to see if she was visibly hurt, but she looked unharmed.

Realization hit Sigurd. He looked at his people. "The gods must have sent her to help us with the fortress."

He did not trust mortal women, but goddesses were another thing altogether.

They nodded, their eyes big and full of wonder. Maybe she, as a goddess, favored him. Maybe she would do magic and bring them strength to finish the fortress by the end of summer. With the number of men they had now, they had no hope.

"Well then, jarl," Asa pressed her fists against her waist. "What are we going to do with her? She looks fine to me at first glance, but I need to examine her properly. And treat her if need be. But imagine what she would think if she woke up on a bench in my house. Floki's feet in her face, chicken poop on the floor, cows mooing. She shouldn't even sleep on a bench in your great hall."

"Why not?" Floki said. "It was good enough for Vigdis her whole life. Even kings sleep there when they visit."

Asa's eyes rounded. "Do you want to offend the gods, Floki?" She turned to Sigurd. "She needs to be in the best place in the whole village so that she feels honored."

Sigurd knew where Asa was leading. But he did not like the thought of a stranger in his bed one bit. Gods, he hated when women were right.

"My bedchamber," Sigurd said. "Indeed, she should feel welcome. We need a miracle to finish the fortress."

Sigurd took the woman in his arms like a precious spoil from a raid and walked towards the village. His skin tingled where her body pressed against his. There might, after all, be nothing wrong with having a goddess in his bed.

CHAPTER THREE

*S*omeone breathed next to Donna.

Strange. This must be a dream. She did not remember going on a date last night. In fact, she couldn't remember much at all, her mind buzzing like a meditation gong.

Good. No thinking now. The aftertaste of something unpleasant that had happened in her waking life lingered in the corners of her psyche like a thief. She wanted to forget it, to make it go away. If this was one of *those* dreams, with a man next to her, she'd better enjoy his company.

She opened her eyes and saw the silhouette of someone big lying with his back to her. A man, indeed.

This was new. Her sexy dreams usually began close to the action—a knight, or a pirate, or even a Japanese samurai—coming in, whispering something sweet in her ear, and taking her like he was starving and she was his last meal. When she was awake, she despised the type. But in the privacy of her fantasies, only a strong, powerful man could set her body on fire.

Donna surveyed the room around her. It was dark, the

only light coming from four lanterns hanging in the corners. A thatched roof sloped high above her head. Axes, swords, and shields hung on the rough plank walls. Three chests stood by the wooden door, which had gaps and offered little privacy. There were no windows. The wind howled outside, and the smell of rain reached her nose.

Not her New York apartment, that was for sure. What a strangely vivid fantasy.

Donna turned on her side, and furs tickled her ankles. She looked under the fur blanket. She had some sort of a linen nightdress on, medieval by the looks of it.

Donna was curious now as to what kind of a guy her subconscious had come up with this time. A Viking by the looks of the room… She reached out to the massive shoulder and ran her fingertips along his shape. The man stirred and slapped her hand as if it was a fly.

Donna frowned. *Ok, dream master, this is too real. Can we sweeten this up, please?*

She slid closer to the man, brushing her hand against his shoulder blade and down the bulging muscles of his back. But before she could reach his buttocks—which would for sure be deliciously firm and round—the man pivoted, pinned her to the mattress and put a knife to her throat.

Donna gasped, adrenaline sending her heart into an erratic beat. The man studied her. Then his face relaxed, and he rolled onto his back. Donna clutched the fur blanket under her chin and crawled into the furthest corner of the bed.

"Goddess, it's you," the man's voice rolled like the purr of a lion. He put the knife aside. "Do not play with a sleeping warrior."

No kidding. Donna swallowed.

As her heart rate began to slow down, she realized that he'd called her a goddess. No way this was reality.

She studied him. He was striking: dark-blond hair, a short beard, eyes the color of the leaden sky. The air buzzed around him, and even though he did not touch her, the aura of his presence tickled her skin like static electricity. No one had ever affected her that way, not even Daniel.

This would do.

Donna breathed out and gave out a chuckle. "You frightened me, too."

As the words came out of her mouth, she knew she spoke a foreign language. But she had no difficulty searching for words or understanding the man. This dream was going to be fun.

"How are you feeling? You lay unconscious since yesterday."

She frowned. "I did? I don't remember how I got here."

"You just appeared. I brought you here. I hope that you find this satisfactory."

"Oh." Donna smiled. "Very. What is your name?"

"Sigurd Randverson. I am the jarl here."

Donna bit her lip. She remembered from history class that a jarl was like an earl. She was in bed with a Viking jarl, and what a handsome one. Anticipation warmed her body. He reached out and brushed her lower lip with his thumb. Her breath quickened. "Welcome. What may I call you, goddess?"

"Donna."

"Donna," he rolled her name on his tongue like candy. His gaze crawled down her body, and her skin tingled. "My beautiful goddess."

Her cheeks heated, his words making her melt like caramel in the sun. The New York woman in her would have already made fun of him—and of herself, for reacting like that.

But that New York woman could take a break.

Donna wrapped her arms around his neck and gently pulled him closer. His scent enveloped her. Fresh sea, pine and the musky scent of man. Oh, she could lose herself completely in him. Her palms crawled down and landed on his bulging chest covered in blond curls. His fingers ran up her forearms and kneaded the muscles of her arms. His hands warmed her and relaxed her.

"Your skin is like silk," he murmured. "This is no skin of a mortal. Will you lie with me, goddess?"

Lie with him? She was ready to sell her soul to spend a night with him.

"Yes."

He tilted his head and sealed his mouth over hers. His firm lips were soft and full of need. They pressed against hers gently. His tongue tasted hers, stroking it gently.

His hands traveled down her legs and pulled the night-dress up over her head until he freed Donna from it. Her naked skin burned with anticipation. His fingers circled her nipples but didn't touch them. Electricity shot through her, her breasts ached pleasantly. Her body writhed against him, impatient for more, the sweet friction making her pliable and warm. She reached for his trousers, but he stopped her.

He lay her down on the mattress and pulled her arms high above her head, locking them with one hand, then came back to her breasts and kneaded them with the other. Her back arched and she pressed herself against his palm. She bit her lip as she tried and failed to hold back a whimper.

"I want you to beg," his coarse voice resonated in her chest.

Oh, it won't take long.

His hand drifted down her side, back down between her legs, fingers teasing. A light brush of his thumb over her clit made her cry out. When he slipped one large finger into her sleekness, a long moan escaped her throat. A second finger entered, working her slower than she wanted, but sending her to a world of sweet agony she'd had no idea existed.

"Does this please you?" Sigurd bent his head to trail a line of nips and delicate licks along her neck, outright biting when he reached her shoulder.

"Ah," she was delirious from pleasure. "This is the best dream I have ever had."

He continued his sweet torture. "A dream? Goddess, if this is a dream, then I am a dwarf of Nidavellir."

Donna was way too hot and way too far gone to fully understand his words.

"Whatever you say...please, don't stop." Her body continued moving in waves against his, but he froze.

"Donna. This is not a dream. You are here, with me, in Norway, in Vörnen."

This was too precise. Donna opened her eyes. He loomed over her with a frown.

She swallowed. "Vörnen, Norway? And you are a Viking jarl?"

"A Norse jarl."

Cold sweat broke out on her skin. What if this wasn't a dream? Still aroused, Donna became aware of her nakedness. She jerked to remove her hands from under his arm and cover herself, but he pinned them against the pillow and pressed her into the mattress.

"Pinch me," she said.

"What?"

"If it's not a dream, it will hurt. Pinch me."

"That is strange logic, goddess,"

He pinched her in the naked side of her waist, and sharp pain mixed with a tickle shot through her.

She froze, her memory returning in an avalanche. The courthouse. Marta. Daniel. Old lady with a spindle. *There is a man who needs you...*

Sleek horror crawled down her spine. She'd just instigated sex with a man she'd only just met.

But more importantly, where was she? What had happened to her? Was she hallucinating? This was too real— and Sigurd's pinch hurt. Was she kidnapped by an accomplice of the old lady? She did not remember anything after touching that spindle. Had she fallen and gotten a concussion? But her head did not hurt.

Wherever she was and whatever had happened to her, an uncontrollable need to run away to safety took over her body and her mind. She had to see outside.

"Let me go, you barbarian!" she writhed as if her life depended on it, kicking him and biting. She had to know. But he was like a mountain.

"No. I am not letting you run away."

"I am not running away. I just need to see where I am. Let me go!"

She was lying. She would run away if she had to.

Still holding her arms, he rose. "Don't think I'll let you out of my sight even for a moment."

Donna nodded. He let her go and went to the door, blocking it. He was still naked from the waist up, and Donna's breath caught in her throat from the mighty sight of him. He was the most magnificent man she had ever seen.

He nodded to one of the chests with his chin. "Here are some clothes for you. The ones you came in are not suitable for our conditions. Maybe they are perfect for your world"— he pointed his finger at the ceiling—"but here, you'll freeze in them. I hid your shoe-weapons in a safe place. I can't trust you."

Donna wanted to laugh. Did he think her stilettos were weapons? This was ridiculous.

She got up, the blanket of furs still wrapped around her to cover her nakedness, and walked to the chests. She opened

21

the one he pointed at and found a long linen shift, a red apron dress with brooches, and soft leather shoes.

"Turn around," she said.

He only raised his eyebrows.

"Turn around, Sigurd."

"I am not letting you out of my sight, goddess. First, I don't trust you yet. Second, I am not going to deny myself the pleasure of seeing your naked body in my own house."

Donna growled. "How dare you treat me like I am your property!"

Sigurd only scoffed.

"Turn around, you self-centered hemorrhoid!"

"A what?"

"I am not changing while you are staring at me."

"Suit yourself. Stay naked forever."

Donna's chin rose, and she pressed her anger down. She needed to see where she was. She had to decide what was more important, her pride or finding out the truth. "Whatever. You want to see me naked? Fine. You already did. I have to see what's outside."

The furs fell in a small pile around her. Sigurd sucked in a breath, and Donna hid a smile. Without looking at him, but with burning cheeks, she dressed. The clothes were surprisingly soft and pleasant against her skin, and the shoes were a little big, but comfortable.

"Let's go," she said.

Sigurd put on a tunic and took an ax. He clasped her elbow, and she shoved him back. "Don't you touch me!"

He only chuckled, "That is not possible, goddess."

He grasped her upper arm even firmer, opened the door, and led her through a giant hall.

Donna eyed everything with an open mouth. The hall was dark, spacious and long. There was a little platform with a giant wooden throne. Fire crackled softly in a long hearth in the center of the room. Along the walls, were benches with people sleeping on them. The columns were decorated with Viking patterns that reminded Donna of the golden spindle. It smelled like hay, and ale, and wood.

It all seemed so real. Her hands started to shake.

They went through the high gates of the hall outside.

It was dawn, and Donna could see wooden longhouses all around her. Down past the village lay the surface of a smooth fjord, several Viking-looking longships were docked at the pier, and mountains rose like walls along its shores. The air was fresh and almost tasted sweet.

It seemed that, by some miracle, Donna was indeed in Norway, in some sort of a medieval village. If she believed in magic, she'd think she'd traveled back in time...

No. Impossible. It must be some sort of reenactment. But how had she gotten here, and how would she get home? Was she a prisoner here? Her vision blackened, the earth shifted under her feet. Her hand searched for something to hold on to and gripped a warm arm.

She glanced at Sigurd, their eyes locked, and the solid strength in his gray gaze steadied her.

"I need to go back."

CHAPTER FOUR

*S*he needed what?

Sigurd's hand stiffened around Donna's elbow. She'd looked like she would faint just now, as if she found herself in an impossible place.

There was something so human in her reaction. She did not seem like a goddess at all. There was a plea in her blue eyes. And panic. And terror.

He gritted his teeth. His muscles were still soaked in the aftertaste of her body against his. He could not remember wanting any woman as much as he wanted her. Everything that he had felt next to her was close to divine. He had thought that, finally, the gods smiled at him.

But if she had no intention to be here, why had the gods sent her? She said she needed to go back. "And where is that?"

"New York," she breathed out.

"Do you mean the town of Jorvik in Northumbria that Ivar the Boneless conquered?"

Her eyes widened even more. "Northumbria? The ancient

24

kingdom that no longer exists? Stop joking around! Everyone has heard of New York."

He raised his eyebrows.

She pressed. "You know, New York? United States of America?"

Sigurd laughed. "Your words are as tangled as Loki's beard. Where is that? Sounds like it could be in Ireland, although I haven't heard of it."

Donna grunted in exasperation and looked at her elbow — which he was still holding. She struggled to free it. "Will you let go of me! I wouldn't know where to run!"

She was so small, but so feisty. "Are you taking me for a fool, goddess?"

Her mouth opened and closed. He smirked. Inspired by an idea, he glanced at the pile of construction materials lying by the high gate of the great longhouse. There were ropes, and without releasing her, he took a short one.

Donna gasped. "You are not—"

Without granting her a response, he drew her to him, letting go of her elbow and wrapping his arms around her, the rope in his hands. Her body was pressed against him and her pupils dilated, soft lips parting. Her sweet scent enveloped him: fresh berries, and wood warmed by the sun, and crisp air high up the mountains, and something else— something out of this world.

Sigurd tied the rope around her waist, finishing with a sea knot. Her eyes opened wider, she gasped and began to struggle, shoving him away, but he held her in place. Her waist was so narrow, so fragile. The memory of her silky skin under his fingers made him swallow, and a jolt of desire shot through him.

"Not a step away from me," his voice rasped.

He let go of her, and she swayed as if she'd lost balance.

"Am I some sort of a *slave* to you? Release me at once! How dare you!"

Donna could not look like slave even if she tried. Rather, she resembled the goddess of storms, her cheeks flushed, her eyes shooting lightning bolts. She even seemed to have grown in height.

But he could not act on his desire now. The fortress had to be built, and he had to know if the goddess could be of any use. Without saying another word, he walked on the dirt path towards the arch, tugging her after him. She dug in her feet like a stubborn goat.

"Where are you taking me?"

"To the stone arch where you appeared. Either the arch or you have special powers, and I am going to find out which."

Donna stopped struggling. Sigurd glanced back at her. She watched everything with big eyes and an open mouth. She was pale and barely looked where she walked. They were passing by other longhouses, what was there to stare at? Maybe Floki's masterful carvings on the beams? He had carved his personal design that distinguished Vörnen from other villages. Yes, they were something to admire, but Donna stared at everything as if she expected trolls and giants from Jötunheimr to spill from the doors and from behind the corners of the houses. It was still early, so only a few people had started their morning duties.

"Is this a movie set?" she asked.

"A what?"

"Why are people dressed as if we are in medieval times? Where are power poles? Why are there no windows on the houses? Those ships," she pointed at the longships down by the beach, behind the unfinished wall of the fortress. "They look pretty historic... There must be some logical explanation. Are you guys some sort of a cult? Or something like the Amish but in Norway?"

Sigurd frowned. Some of her words made no sense. "Are you attempting to cast a spell, goddess?"

"Stop with the 'goddess' already, please! Let me think. I am a rational person. I was in a courthouse with my clients and Daniel, and then there was that old lady… Wait. You said I just appeared. Under that arch, right? What happened exactly?"

Courthouse? Clients? It was as if she was from a different world altogether. "Floki, his wife Asa and I were raising a palisade. The stake fell on the wall of the arch, and you appeared."

They approached the archway, which stood a few dozen feet away from the last house, hidden behind the grove of trees. The rock that had almost killed Donna still lay on the ground.

Sigurd pointed at it. "This is right where you appeared yesterday."

Donna's eyes traveled around the arch, her eyes wide. "This is in the middle of nowhere. Even the fjord is far away, so I couldn't come by sea. There are trees all around, a helicopter would not be able to land. Did they just drop me? But I don't feel pain anywhere. How could I just appear?"

A helicopter? Was that a type of dragon the goddess might have been riding? Sigurd looked for any signs of magic that she might be experiencing being next to the arch. The only magic he sensed was his accelerated heartbeat caused by her presence. "Do you feel anything?" he asked.

"I feel that you are hurting me." She tugged at the rope around her waist.

Sigurd loosened the knot a little. His fingers melted where they touched her waist. Why did she have such an effect on him? He was burning for her.

This was no good. He could not give her this power over him.

27

He swallowed and pressed. "Any magic? Can you make the stone rise?"

Donna snorted. "Please."

She walked away from him towards the rock, and disappointment stung in his chest because she left his side. She circled the stone, her steps gracious, her gentle curves moving under the clothes. The rope stretched, and he yanked her back slightly. She rewarded him with a furious glance.

Even though Sigurd had brought her here, he did not like her sniffing around the rocks one bit. What if she disappeared the same way she had appeared? Or worse, what if she took a rock and smashed him later in his sleep? "What are you looking for?"

"I don't know. Any signs of a logical explanation. A gag treated with chloroform. A hidden door. A mirror box." She froze and glanced up at him. "Wait. You said Asa was with you? Is she old and does she have a golden spindle?"

"A golden spindle? Asa is not rich enough to have such a treasure. Even I don't own gold anymore."

A jarl needed treasure to keep his warriors' loyalty. Sigurd had given all of his gold away to retain the last strong warriors when his father had gotten sick, and since then they had not gone on a single raid. The gold was gone, and only silver remained. It was disappearing quickly too as he paid the remaining men. He could only hope they would be able to go on raids next year, once the fortress was built.

All of these misfortunes because of a woman's betrayal...

Sigurd frowned, something Donna had said catching his attention.

A golden spindle. And an old woman... Could it be... "Where did you see the old woman with the spindle?"

"In the courthouse in New York. She came to me and said a man needed me, and then she asked me to hold her golden spindle. There were patterns carved on it, they looked like the ones on your columns. She was knitting a scarf with a tree."

A tree? Could it be the Yggdrasil, the tree of the world? "The only being who has a golden spindle is one of three Norns."

"Three Norns? Who are they?"

"They spin the threads of people's fates. And gods' fates. They define when we are born, when we die, and what happens to us. A scald that visited my hall—back when my father was the jarl—sung a legend in which the three Norns had a golden, a silver, and a bronze spindle."

Donna's eyebrows crawled up. Sigurd glanced at the arch. It had always looked like it was more than just a strange collection of rocks piled up together. It must be. He wished now that they had a priest or a witch in the village, someone who knew seidr, the art of magic and witchcraft. They'd know about the arch.

But even Sigurd, who was not a witcher, could feel something powerful beyond words in those rocks. So it was no surprise that someone like Donna would appear here. When they completed the fortress and regained their strength as a jarldom, it would be the perfect place for a sacred grove. The gods would love the arch.

The Norn surely did if she'd sent Donna here.

Donna shook her head and turned around, walking towards the arch. The rope stretched, and he felt like a troll that caught a struggling fish. He yanked her back. He did not want her to touch the sacred stones. The arch could be the portal through which she came.

"Do not go near it."

Donna clasped her hands in exasperation but then glanced at him suspiciously. "Why?"

"Because I said so."

"I don't believe this nonsense. I am a New York lawyer,

for God's sake. There is no such thing as Norns and there's no such thing as magic."

But as she was saying this, her words trailed off. Sigurd crossed his arms over his chest. She did not believe in magic? Lies. He grabbed her by the elbow and spun her around to face him.

Her face was a mask of fury, her breasts pressed against him sending heat through his muscles like the strongest mead.

She was so close, he inhaled the sweet scent of her breath. The urge to kiss her made his head spin.

"I don't give a Loki's turd what you believe. You are here because the most powerful being in all worlds wants you here. With me. Now. Stop acting like a confused simpleton and do something about the fortress!"

CHAPTER FIVE

"*I* can't!"

Donna had never felt like this in her life. Disbelief in the only logical—yet impossible—explanation tore her mind apart like a high fever. Sigurd's mountain of a body and his furious face intimidated her despite her attempts to feel strong and confident. His hard muscles pressed against her made her heart race and her skin buzz with sweet anticipation. He was so close she could kiss him. But damned if she would ever allow that to happen again.

She needed to find the way back.

His eyes went ice-cold. "You can't?"

She swallowed. "I am not a goddess." She could not believe what she was about to say out loud. "I am a regular woman. From the future."

As she heard her own words, she snorted right in his face. He blinked, and a giggle escaped her, brought on by his astonishment, the silliness of snorting in a huge Viking's face, and the ridiculousness of what was going on in her head. Then a full shower of laughter poured out of her. Hysteria. Her belly tensed, ached and shook.

She must have gone insane.

Sigurd let go of her and wiped his face with his palm, his eyebrows knit together. Donna doubled up, trying to breathe deeply to calm herself down, but little giggles burst out of her.

"Are you done?"

Donna breathed out the remains of hysteria and nodded. "Sorry for that." She circled with her index finger around his face.

He grunted.

"Why are you not freaking out, Sigurd? It sounds insane. It's the craziest thing I have ever said in my life."

She felt the weight of Sigurd's eyes on her. "A woman from the future." His gaze traveled up and down her body, and despite herself, heat pulsed through her, making her skin tingle. "How do you know?"

She almost choked from the ridiculousness of his question. "The axes, wooden houses without electricity, the way you are dressed, the ships, the technology—she pointed at the stake lying on the ground—It's all so medieval. Plus, the fact that I magically started to speak and understand Norwegian—or whatever the equivalent was back then." She frowned. "Is...now."

Ha. She was arguing for the opposite side.

"Do you use shoes as weapons in the future?"

She chuckled, "No, they are just for walking. Beauty. The world is a more peaceful place a thousand or so years from now. Well, relatively. Most people don't need weapons. My mom and I—"

Oh no. Her mom. She must be sick with worry. Who would help Donna's four clients? Her mom could not juggle her own cases and Donna's case, which was the biggest their little firm had ever had.

"You don't believe me, do you?"

"Oh, I believe you. Norns can do that. That must be Skuld," he said, and Donna understood that Skuld was a name that meant "What Shall Be."

"She is the one who rules destiny across time. What I can't understand is, why you?"

Donna's eyebrows rose. The fact that he believed her without questioning shocked her, and she eyed him, looking for a sign that he was joking. A modern man would doubt her words. But he was no modern man. That was another nail in the coffin of her hope.

"I don't know! She made a mistake. I have no clue what I can do to help you. But I need to get back, Sigurd!"

"You can't."

The words hit her like rocks. "What?"

Sigurd's brows snapped together. "There's no way back when a Norn wants you here."

Donna's chest tensed. *No way back...* Even though she was in the open, she felt as if she was in a shoebox. She often felt close to a panic attack in small spaces, elevators or the subway. She'd had that feeling ever since she was four years old.

Donna had woken up in the middle of the night to screams and the bangs of furniture hitting the walls. Her mother argued with her then-boyfriend, Joseph, a litigator in the same prestigious law firm. Donna's heart raced, she ran towards the door to go to her mom, but the door would not open. The apartment was old-fashioned, and the doors had locks on the outside. Without her mother's knowledge, the man liked to lock Donna's door so she wouldn't bother them when he spent the night. She had spent the remains of that night curled in a ball, with her hands pressed against her ears and her eyes shut so she wouldn't see the walls of her tiny Manhattan bedroom close in on her.

Several years later, Donna found out that was the night

he'd told her mother he had gotten her promotion to junior partner.

Being trapped here felt just like that night for Donna. Her hands shook, and her chest started to hurt. No. She could not have a panic attack. Not now.

"I need to go back, Sigurd. People rely on me there. Four women and their children could lose everything—and most likely land on the streets."

His jaw muscles flexed. He pointed at the ditch. "If we don't build the fortress, the whole village could die. And you are here to prevent that, even though you are just a woman. Maybe if you are from the future, you are different. So, forgive me if I am not in a hurry to help you get back."

Donna gasped. *"Just a woman?* Are you serious? And, excuse me, how am I here to prevent the village from dying?"

"I am building a fortress around the village. I need to finish before the end of summer, and the fortress does not rise fast enough. What can you do? Are you a builder?"

Donna glanced at the stake. "No."

"Can you craft?"

"No."

"Can you at least fight?"

"I took a class on self-defense with a badass woman with a burned face. And I go to Krav Maga twice a week."

"Does Krav Maga involve swords and axes?"

"No."

"Then it's not going to help in a battle. How will you help?"

Donna looked around at the ditch, the fallen stake, and the arch. Desperation made her feet heavy and her hands weak. "I don't know! Ask your Norn."

"What is it that you do, exactly, in your time?"

Did the Vikings even have the concept of a lawyer? "I

protect the rights of women who were treated badly. By men, by their employers, by the government."

"This sounds ridiculous. If someone wrongs a woman, it's the duty of her husband, her father, or her brothers, to avenge her. Not the task of another woman. Besides, no mortal female can be trusted with such an important thing as the law. What can you know about it?"

Anger simmered in her, and Donna took a deep breath to calm down. These were barbarian times, she reminded herself. "I will have you know that in a bit over a thousand years, women will have as many rights as men. Officially, anyway. Unofficially, they are often treated like they are in your times."

Sigurd leaned towards her, and she held her breath. His hands untied the knot of the rope around her waist, sending waves of electricity through her skin.

"You are useless for the fortress. Just keep out of the way. Since you came through the arch, it must be the doorway. You might be able to go back through it. The arch will be rebuilt because it's an important part of the defenses, not because of you. And then, whether you go or stay does not interest me. But do not dare touch anything. Keep yourself busy with womanly work: help with cooking and cleaning. Don't talk to anyone. Go back to the longhouse. If you are hungry, you may eat. If you need to relieve yourself, you may go to the outhouse."

Donna gasped for breath from all the insults. Womanly work... Keep out of the way... Like she was some sort of a slave!

Sigurd walked off in the direction of the village, leaving her alone. "Be in my bedchamber by nightfall. I am not finished with you there yet," he threw back over his shoulder.

CHAPTER SIX

*D*onna stood for a moment, her mouth opening without a sound, shock and anger boiling in her stomach like water in a kettle, but there was also something else, something she forbade herself to feel. Her deep muscles throbbed as the image of Sigurd's naked body over hers flooded her imagination.

No. No! She could not act on these feelings. Yes, she was attracted to him, but Sigurd and she did not have any future whatsoever. He was exactly the type she had decided to stay clear of since Daniel. And—most importantly—she did not belong here and needed to go back. She, a New York lawyer, with a Viking! She scoffed, but the thought did not sound as ludicrous as she wanted it to.

Stop thinking about him and start acting!

Even though Donna knew it would probably be futile, she walked towards the arch and lay her hands on it. The rocks were cold and rough, lifeless. She even squeezed her eyes shut, hoping that she'd open them in New York.

But nothing happened.

Darn it. She was really stuck here.

She looked around, and her chest tightened as if clenched in a vise, as the trees began closing in on her like those walls of her Manhattan bedroom. Donna ran to the village.

The settlement was wide awake by now, people busy with their morning work, faces stern. Men walked towards the sides of the village, probably to continue building the fortress. Women hurried cows, sheep, and goats out in the pastures with "hey" and "tsk tsk tsk." Children helped by carrying hay, vegetables, and buckets of water. Chickens cackled, and geese honked. The smell of fresh manure mingled with the sweet air, but it was not disturbing. It was strangely comforting.

From a distance, Donna saw Sigurd walk out of the longhouse. She hoped he'd see her, but he walked off towards the center of the village. Fully armed with a shield, a battle ax, and a sword, he looked glorious, like an ancient warlord.

Breath caught in her throat at the sight of him. Where was he headed? If Donna wanted to go back, she needed to have the arch repaired. And for that, she needed Sigurd to do something now, not whenever he got around to it. Donna followed him.

Sigurd stopped at a small square where a dozen or so teenage boys with wooden axes, swords, and shields battled each other in mock fights. Sigurd yelled "Shieldwall!" and they dashed towards each other, building three rows of shields. Donna's throat caught at the thought that these adolescents—these children—were training for war. Sigurd barked commands, and they grouped, regrouped, fought with each other, and with him. He corrected them, praised them and gave them bruises. They watched him as if he were a god.

And he looked like one. Who was the god of battle? Thor, wasn't he? Well, it might as well have been Sigurd.

For the first time since she'd arrived, she had a moment

to think and really wonder what sort of man he was. He must certainly be a great warrior, a strong man, and a good leader if he cared so much about his people that he had put everything on the line to build the fortress. He worked with his own hands alongside his people—he'd said he was building the palisade with Floki and Asa when she'd appeared there. And now, he was taking personal care to make sure these boys stood a chance against whatever enemy threatened them. He seemed to be a good man. Her heart squeezed and warmth spread through her.

No, she should not allow these feelings. That was all good and nice, but he was still a discriminating, stubborn, arrogant—

Someone grabbed her wrist and spun her around. A Viking she had not seen before loomed over her. He was younger than Sigurd, and shorter, less impressively built. A violent curiosity was written all over his face. Fear gripped her throat.

"Are you the goddess that fell from the sky yesterday?"

Donna tried to free her arm, but the man was as strong as an ox. She should kick his butt, but she did not want to escalate the situation. "Get off me!"

He wore a homespun tunic, though his was older than Sigurd's, and he reeked of stale sweat.

"You don't look like a goddess. You look like a Freyja's whore."

Donna gasped, and the hair stood on her nape and arms. He pulled her towards him. "You better come with me," he whispered wetly into her ear. "Fulfill your destiny."

That was it. She'd had enough. Donna swung up the arm he was holding her with. He lost his advantage as his arm suddenly was raised high. Using his confusion, she grabbed his wrist with both hands, twisting his arm into a straight line and making him turn with his back to her. Then she pushed on his straight arm and he fell to one knee on the ground, growling in pain.

"Maggots in Loki's skull," Sigurd's voice behind Donna rolled like thunder.

She glanced back at Sigurd, and the shock written on his face was priceless. Donna smirked internally. Self-defense and Krav Maga had paid off. If she could force a Viking to his knees, she could deal with whatever else this time-travel nightmare had to dish up.

"Geirr, you just put your hands on another man's woman. But I see she does not need her man to protect her."

Donna's skin tingled at the look of respect in Sigurd's eyes.

"Let me go, you wench!" Geirr moaned. "Jarl, I did not know she was claimed."

Sigurd stopped next to her. "She is claimed. By me."

Donna's breath caught. A forbidden thrill went through her. His words sounded so wrong and so primal, but, oh God, it made her want to throw herself into his arms and let him show her exactly how he claimed her.

"Let him go, Donna. He won't harm you. No one will."

She released Geirr, and he rose, facing them and eyeing Sigurd from under his heavy brows.

Sigurd gave a curt nod. "Should you not be at the fortress?"

The man backed away and disappeared behind the corner of the next building.

Sigurd slowly turned Donna around. He loomed over her like the mountain over the fjord, his eyes as gray. But they were not full of desire as Donna had secretly hoped.

They were full of fury.

CHAPTER SEVEN

*O*din and Thor, she was trouble.

He had thought maybe women from the future were different, more trustworthy. They had clearly been given greater responsibility. But a small woman like her had brought one of his best warriors to his knees with just a couple of clever movements.

Sigurd was furious. At her, but mostly at himself.

He should have been more careful with her, should have just locked her up and posted guards to make sure she would not wander around the village, confusing his men, creating chaos, and distracting him.

But he had no men to spare and no time to lose.

As she stood so close to him—her eyes big, her lips full and juicy like ripe cherries begging him to kiss them, her scent enveloped him.

He'd told Geirr he'd claimed her.

Right now, he did not want anything more than to do just that. To take her, make her his, plunge into her scent like he plunged into the waters of the fjord, forget himself in her arms and find release in her depths.

Sigurd swallowed and looked up to distract himself. He needed to get her under control and get back to work on the fortress.

He walked towards the great hall and pulled her after him. "I told you not to talk to anyone."

Donna's eyes widened. "He came to me! He grabbed me and—"

Sigurd growled. "I told you to go to the longhouse. Just stay there. Do not take a step outside."

They arrived in his great hall, and Donna started to struggle, but he led her towards his bedchamber, ignoring the curious glances of the slaves.

When they were in his bedchamber, Donna pulled her arm from his grip and spun to face him, her eyes a blue fury in the darkness of the room.

"You are such a dictator! You have no right to tell me what to do. And what about that thing you said about claiming me? No one—you hear me—no one can claim me! I belong to myself. I claim me. I claim… "

Sigurd did not know half of what she was talking about. Dictator? What was that?

"I have every right to do anything I see fit with you. You are under my protection."

Donna scowled and crossed her arms. Freyja and Frigg, her lips looked so kissable right now.

"Make yourself useful and help with cooking and cleaning, like I told you."

Her chin rose. "And warming your bed?"

He swallowed and glanced at the object in question, which was full of soft furs and so inviting. "And warming my bed."

Donna drew in a sharp breath. "You can forget it."

Sigurd took a step towards her. Would she fight him in everything? "I don't think that I can." His hand rose to her face and he traced the gentle curve of her cheek.

Her skin felt like that of a goddess. No woman he had ever met had skin like that. Her sweet lips parted slightly at his touch. She could say whatever she wanted, but she was affected as much as he was.

Before the voice in his head could roar at him to stop and walk out, he lowered his head towards her. He needed to claim her, Sigurd said to himself, before she could create more havoc.

But he knew it was just an excuse.

The real reason was this.

His lips touched hers, and she welcomed him as if he was a long-lost part of her. She moaned, barely audible, and her body pressed against him. He breathed her in, his tongue ravishing hers, the sweet taste of her mouth making him crave her even more.

He picked her up and carried her to the bed. He sat on the edge and placed her on his lap, turning her so that her legs wrapped around his hips. Her body pressed against his, her soft breasts and belly—her heat against his. Their eyes locked, and there was hunger in hers that mirrored his own. But also the shadow of doubt.

No, there would be none of that now. No thoughts, no questions, no hesitation.

His lips covered hers before the doubt could win her over. He tangled one hand in her hair as he let the other travel down her graceful spine, trace the hemisphere of her backside and move down her thigh, before slipping under the hem of her dress where it had gathered right above her knees. His fingers glided along her smooth skin.

She felt like a goddess, but he knew now that she was just a woman...and what a willful woman she was. He rolled her hair on his fist and pulled her head back a little, exposing her graceful neck to his mouth. He kissed it, devouring every inch of the skin. Then he reached a spot just below her ear, bit it gently, and Donna gave a throaty cry of pleasure. She was strangely connected to him. He did not know how, but he felt what she wanted, what would make her feel good.

And he was happy to oblige.

Sigurd's hands slid under her hips, supporting her, and he rose up with her. He turned to the bed and threw Donna on it, joining her right after. Her lips were full, her mouth parted, her eyes half-closed. Sigurd leaned over her with his arms straight, pushing against the mattress at each side of her shoulders. He knelt between her legs. She gasped a little, her legs spread, at his mercy. She bit her lip, and her head rolled back slightly, their eyes still locked. Sigurd lowered himself to her, pinning her to the mattress. He grasped her wrists in one hand, pulling her arms above her head, wanting to finish what they'd started that morning.

Donna wriggled a little, rubbing herself against him. He kissed her again, and she moaned against his mouth.

Sigurd was pressed against her completely now, throbbing and hard, at her hot entrance. His mouth found hers and devoured her. Her body began grinding itself shamelessly against his.

Sigurd undid her brooches and ran his hand down her leg, then returned to the hem of the dress. He lifted for a moment, pulling her dress over her head and off. Her milky white body lay before him, her full breasts, delicate waist, round hips. Her skin...oh her skin... And the triangle of light-brown hair between her thighs.

Sigurd groaned. And then he was surprised to feel her hands on his waist, pulling at his tunic and trying to raise it up.

He glanced at her, and she whispered, "Why should you do all the work?"

The tunic flew to the floor. Then her fingers reached for

the rope tying his trousers together and touched the skin on his stomach, so close to his erection. Both electricity and a jolt of panic shot through Sigurd, and his cock jerked. He never allowed a bedmate to give him oral pleasure. He just could not give a woman that control over him. He needed to be careful. What was she going to do?

Her fingers touched him. Intense pleasure spread through him. Sigurd clenched his fists and had to call on all his strength to not throw himself on her and take her. He let her explore his length, play with it, but he would not last long. Did she even know how wild she made him feel?

Donna looked up at him and licked her lips, making a movement to go down, but alarm shot through him, and his hands gripped hers. She blinked in surprise, and he put her palms back on his chest.

He imagined his shaft in her mouth, her tongue teasing him, sliding up and down, and he hardened even more.

But he wouldn't allow it. This is what it always would be. A fantasy.

He pushed her further back along the bed, pressing his body over hers and nudging her legs further open as he trailed hot kisses along her neck.

He pulled back slightly before sliding into her slowly, watching her. She was so sleek and hot, so tight. Her head rolled back as he drove into her inch by inch, and she gave a low moan of pleasure. Freyr, she was so beautiful it was hard to believe she was mortal.

When he was fully encased in her tight core, he had a strange feeling of being home. If he had not been so turned on, he'd have stopped. But he could not.

The only thing he could do was move.

He plunged into her and pulled back, slowly at first, then faster. Her legs wrapped around his waist, bringing him impossibly close, making him feel as if they were one.

She moaned and cried and begged for him not to stop, to never stop.

"I do not intend to," he groaned.

He took her nipple in his mouth and sucked, and she arched her back to give him better access.

He moved faster and faster, knowing his release would come soon and not wanting it to. But she was close, too.

With a few final hard thrusts, he felt her insides quiver, and she breathed quickly, erratically, and gave out the sweetest cries of ecstasy. She sent him over the edge, and he spilled in her, making her truly his.

As he collapsed on her after the most intense orgasm of his life, Sigurd felt their chests rise and fall in unison and her silky body in his arms. And for the first time he did not want to let a woman go.

CHAPTER EIGHT

 hen Donna woke up next morning, Sigurd was gone, and the bed chilled her skin without his warmth. Yesterday she had experienced, undoubtedly, the most mind-blowing sex of her life. Her body felt sated and alive, as if every cell had been awoken after a long sleep. As she stretched, a quiet, primal rhythm beat in her very core and gave her strength and energy. She could not quite believe she had given in to Sigurd, but if she ever got back to New York, she'd think back on this as if it was a little adventure, a once-in-a-lifetime experience.

Right. New York. Home. She needed to find a way back. The thought sobered her up, and she quickly dressed.

Was Sigurd still somewhere in the great hall? Donna opened the door and surveyed the giant room, but he was not there. He must be at the construction site.

Women in simple clothes did housework: cooking at the long hearth, sweeping the floors, sewing. Traditional gender roles. Donna shook her head but reminded herself this was not her battle. Thank goodness she lived in the twenty-first century.

Donna approached a woman who sliced carrots and threw them into a cauldron that smelled of stew and made Donna's mouth water and her stomach growl.

The woman glanced at Donna. "Ah, Goddess." She gestured at the place on the bench next to her. "You seem better. Did you want to eat?"

Donna frowned. "I'm not a goddess."

The woman eyed her up and down. Her face was weathered, reddish and dry, wrinkles deep. Yet her eyes gave away a younger person, and her hair shone like gold. "You *do* seem like a mortal to me."

Donna chuckled. "And as a mortal, I am, actually, very hungry and thirsty. Where can I find something to eat?"

The woman looked around the room. "Hilde! Bring something for our guest to eat. And don't forget the mead."

A young woman with a short haircut, in clothes that reminded Donna of a sack, nodded and hurried to the furthest corner of the room.

"My name is Asa." The woman returned to her carrots. "Do you have a name?"

"Donna. Are you the Asa who saw me appear by the arch?"

"Just the one. How did you get here? Jarl thinks you came here to help us with the fortress."

Donna swallowed. What did Sigurd want people to know about her? What would be safe to share with Asa, who seemed friendly enough? "It's a long story."

Asa raised her brows but did not pursue the question, and Donna was thankful. She looked around. While many women worked, some seemed to chat while doing their chores leisurely. There wasn't a single man in the hall.

Hilde came with a bowl and a wooden cup that smelled of honey. Donna thanked her and drank the mead. It was delicious. Sweet and cold, only slightly alcoholic, it refreshed her. Her tongue tickled as tiny bubbles went down her throat. Her head buzzed a little. She began to eat, but the food—a combination of cheese and yogurt with oatmeal—was not as good. It was a bit salty and pungent. Still, it was food.

"Why isn't there enough of a workforce?" Donna asked through a full mouth.

Asa's knife froze for a moment, then continued its *chop, chop, chop* but slower. "Last year's raid took the lives of many men—at least half. The old jarl's, too. But the enemy retreated with their tail between their legs. And now all men are working on the fortress, every single one of them. We are in a hurry to raise it by the end of the summer so that next raiding season we have protection against our biggest enemy, even though there are fewer men."

Chills ran down Donna's spine. These were harsh times. While war, violence and death still tore apart countries and communities in her own time, they had, so far, been at a distance—on TV or social media. She couldn't imagine that half of the male population of Brooklyn would suddenly die like the men had in this village. Her chest tightened.

"Let me guess. Sigurd does not employ women to work on the fortress."

Asa's eyes met Donna's. "He does not."

Donna rose to her feet, an idea lightening her mood. Oh, so Sigurd did not want women to help. But he didn't have enough men, and some women did not seem to have important things to do.

"But he could ask you ladies to help, couldn't he? That would give him enough workforce, right?"

Asa shot a sideways glance at her. "Yes, it would."

Donna knew now why the Norn had sent her here. Her inner discrimination lawyer sang. She fought for women's equal rights, and Sigurd was discriminating.

"Asa, could you please gather the women here for me?"

Asa frowned. "Why?"

"Because I am here to help with the fortress."

Asa squinted, then a little smile put dimples in her cheeks. She nodded and put the knife on the cutting board. Then she went around the room calling for women and gesticulating towards Donna, and they began gathering around her. Soon, there were thirty or so women. Some had come in from outside; all watched her with curiosity.

Donna's stomach quivered. What if she was wrong? Was she really assuming she could intervene in the lives of the villagers? She was an outsider, someone from a different time.

But no. If she could bring a positive change, this would be it.

She cleared her throat and imagined she was in front of a jury because the jury usually liked her. "How many of you want to see your families and neighbors alive and well?"

The women nodded and exchanged glances, murmuring approval.

"How many of you think that the men won't be able to finish the fortress by the next raiding season?"

The women's eyes widened with fear now, and their voices rang louder.

"Jarl Sigurd needs more hands. Is the work on defenses not more important than scrubbing that pot till it shines? Would it be so bad to let the floor stay a little dusty if it meant that your brother or husband or son would live and breathe next year?"

She looked around the room, making a point of stopping to meet the eyes of every woman. "Here is what I suggest. Every single one of you who can spare a few hours to go and build the fortress with the men, come with me."

The women stood silent.

"Jarl Sigurd forbade us to touch the fortress," Asa said.

"Did he say why?"

"He said, women can't do important things right."

Donna shook her head. "Sigurd is so wrong! Women can't do important things? Look at you! You are doing them all day long! Cooking, taking care of children and animals, making sure everything is in order… I'd like to see the men left without your work for one day."

They murmured.

"If we don't help, no one will. And if no one will, there will be no one to protect."

Asa nodded. "You are right, Donna. We have strong arms. Each of us can help much. There are more of us than all the men combined. The jarl must see that."

The women were nodding and cheering now. Donna smiled. "Let's go! Asa, lead the way."

They walked through the village towards the fjord, calling for other women that they saw along the way to join them, and by the time they arrived at the construction site that bordered the beach, their numbers had doubled.

The men were busy. They carried logs, chopped branches from the trunks of the trees, dug the ditch, sharpened the logs to make stakes, and planted the stakes in the ditch. The palisade wall was then caked with mud, and from behind, supported by logs that were planted in the ground at an angle. A wooden watchtower stood a few feet to the left, but it lacked a roof.

Once the men saw them, they stopped their work and scowled.

Donna walked on. "Asa, who is the foreman?"

Asa waved to a man. "Thorsten! We are here to help with construction."

"Did the jarl really approve of this?" he said when he approached them.

"Jarl needs help, he's got help," Asa said.

He hesitated, throwing glances at the palisade and back to the women. "Jarl will skin me."

"Good. You won't see your wife and daughters raped and killed."

His face reddened, his eyes bulged.

Donna intervened. "Just give us the simplest tasks."

His gaze lay heavily on her. Finally, he nodded. "Fine. If the goddess thinks so, maybe he'll change his mind. You five, go cut the branches from those trunks. You three, sharpen the edges of those logs. Amba, take six women to bring mud and hay and mix them for the caking..."

The women nodded and rushed to do what Thorsten told them. The men watched them with stern faces.

Asa and Donna approached two men standing next to a log and got into position to lift it with them. On a count of three, they raised it, and the effort knocked the breath out of Donna. She was grateful now for the Krav Maga classes that gave her strength and resilience.

Time flew, and when Sigurd's roar hit the air like a slap, Donna shuddered. She was in the middle of carrying another log together with three other women, and they stopped, carefully laying the log on the ground.

Donna turned around. Sigurd's eyes circled the construction site, his eyebrows knit together and his nostrils flared. Oh, he was glorious, all danger and muscles and passion, and a thrill ran through Donna's body. His gaze locked on her, and heat struck Donna's cheeks. He loped towards her as if she were prey, and Donna ignored an urge to run and hide. When he stopped in front of her, he watched her as if no one and nothing else existed—just like last night when he'd been inside of her. Donna's lips parted, desire to be taken by him spilling through her veins like lava.

"Loki, take me to Helheim, what is this?" Sigurd growled, and Donna gulped down her breath.

Why was he so tall? It was so hard to fight him when he always loomed over her. Her chin rose. "We came to build—"

He took a step closer and she took one back, but they stood half an inch apart, and the heat from his big body warmed her skin. "What did I tell you? Do not take a step out of the longhouse! Do not talk to anyone!"

"Oh, you would forbid me everything if you could! But you are convinced that I came here to help you finish the fortress in time." She gestured around herself. "So there it is. My help."

Sigurd grabbed her by the arm, and his touch sent a wave of desire through her. "This is no help. Women can't construct the fortress."

Donna snatched her arm back from his grip, and a part of her sank in disappointment from breaking the contact. But only a small part. Because he was being a stubborn ass again, one who would get them all killed. And she had to stop him. She stabbed her finger at the fortress. "Constructing. That is *exactly* what they are doing."

If only he could see that! Since the female task force had joined the construction, the number of logs and stakes had tripled, the palisade had been caked with mud, and skilled builders, freed from simple tasks, had started working on the roof of the watchtower.

Sigurd bared his teeth. "Everything here needs to be checked and rechecked, and redone. You doubled the amount of work for the men."

Donna gasped. She itched to kick him. "Are you kidding me? We did simple things—anyone can do them!"

"How many fortresses have you built, Donna? Or you, Asa? Or any of these women? None." He turned to the construction site. "That's it. There will be no more help from the women! If any of you even touch the fortress, you will be banned from my jarldom. Does everyone hear me? *Banned!*" He turned to her. "And you." His eyes pierced her, and her stomach flipped. "Tonight, you'll be sorry for what you did."

CHAPTER NINE

*S*igurd growled from fury and frustration on the way to his bedchamber after a hard day of work. It was good that he'd had to work physically the whole day, otherwise he'd need to start a fight because he itched to punish someone. The stubborn female drove him crazy. She'd almost started an open resistance against him. But, despite himself, he could not help but to admire that she'd managed to make Asa and Thorsten side with her, and convince practically all women of the village to act against their jarl.

She had a nerve.

A nerve, and a brain, and a tongue.

He was looking forward to teaching her a lesson.

The bedchamber was empty.

Disappointment hit him like a blow to the gut, then worry knit his eyebrows together. Where was she? He walked through the great hall, but she was nowhere to be seen. Muffled giggles and moans ran across the darkness: warriors had fun with their bed slaves on the benches.

Servants and thralls were cleaning after dinner. She could not have gone back to her time, could she?

Sigurd's stomach knotted. What had she gotten herself into? If one of his men wanted to repeat Geirr's mistake— He ground his teeth, scorching heat flushed through his body as he imagined another man's hands on her, and his fists clenched so tight, his fingers ached.

He checked that his ax hung on his belt and walked outside. It was still bright; the days of early summer lasted as long as the song of a lousy scald. He went around the village, almost calling her name. As the prospect of her leaving became real, his stomach roiled and icy sweat broke through his skin. He sped up to a trot, and every time he looked behind a house, his pulse jumped in anticipation of seeing her figure. But each time she was not there, his chest tightened more and more until it began to hurt.

After a while, Sigurd ended up at the beach. And through the part unobscured by the palisade, he saw her figure facing the water. It was her, he recognized her even from a distance. Relief flooded him, and he began breathing easier.

Sigurd approached Donna and stood by her side.

"I looked for you," he said after a while.

"Oh, you thought you'd find me warming your bed, did you?"

Sigurd gritted his teeth. "That's what I told you to do."

She turned to him, her face stiff with anger. "Oh yes? And of course, I must obey. Why?"

Was it strange to think she looked glorious when she was so angry? Her eyes shone, full lips pressed together, cheeks flushed. If she'd had a sword in her hand, she might have looked like Brunhild, the legendary shield-maiden.

He suppressed the urge to take her by the shoulders and cover that willful mouth with his.

He turned to face her. Why should she obey him? Well that was obvious. "I am the jarl."

"You are not *my* jarl. You are no one to me." Even though it was true, the words stung. She continued, "Ah. Wait. Of course. I should obey you because I am a *woman*!"

Sigurd studied her. She sounded like his sister. Vigdis had often complained that if she were a man, she'd already have been on raids, on negotiations, hunted with kings and jarls and had her own ship.

He clenched his fists. This was the same beach where he had learned of Vigdis's betrayal. The same beach where his father and many more great warriors had parted with their lives because of her.

And now Donna. Same words. Same attitude.

He ran his fingers through his hair. "A woman," he spat. "Indeed, you are a woman. I learned painfully that I could never trust one. I thought you were different because the Norn sent you to me." He eyed her up and down. "But I was wrong."

Hurt and confusion distorted her face. "What?"

"All you want is power, isn't it? To have a say at the great table, make decisions, and rule."

"What are you talking about? I want to make decisions about me. To be in charge of *my* life. To be equal with men. Not to be regarded as a property."

Sigurd shook his head. "And just what are you prepared to do to gain all these privileges?"

He heard the venom in his own voice, poisonous as the Midgard Serpent—the snake that coiled around the center of the world.

Donna studied him with a frown. "They shouldn't be privileges. And I am ready to fight for that. To never give up."

"To betray. Backstab. Lie—"

Sigurd shut his mouth before he could say anything more

that would open his wound. He groaned. Anger and hurt boiled in his throat and threatened to spill from him in a tidal wave.

Donna watched him, wide-eyed. "Backstab and lie? I would never—" She was silent for a moment, and he almost craved for her to go on, to pull the information out of him like a rotten tooth. "You are not talking about me, are you?"

Her voice brushed him like fur. Tenderness gave her more power than any force.

He swallowed a painful knot. "No."

"What happened?"

He looked at her, searching for the final push that would tip him over the edge and make him talk. The desire to tell her about the most painful experience of his life itched like an old battle wound. Why did he feel he could confide in her? Why did he want to share with her that pain?

Maybe because she was an outsider. And a bit like a goddess.

Or maybe there was just something about her that made his world brighter and more hopeful.

She eyed him as if waiting for his next step. In her eyes, he saw pain that resembled his own.

And then he let go.

"It's my sister. She married our enemy instead of negotiating peace. I entrusted her with the task, even though my father told me his whole life not to trust women.

"I did not want to believe he was right. I resisted. I thought maybe it was just him, that he was stuck in the old ways.

"My father often said that he could not rely on my mother in anything. She had weak health and was often in bed instead of managing the household. She lost many children, and he wanted many sons. For a long time, I was the only child.

"Still, I think he loved her. He forbade her to have any more children, too afraid that she'd die, and she promised him that she wouldn't, that she'd take herbs. But she wanted to be a good wife. And a good wife gives her husband many sons.

"Once, when father raided overseas, a wealthy merchant came to the village. I saw them in the washhouse—back then I thought they wrestled. After he left, she soon began feeling sick. The same kind of sick she felt every time before her belly would swell.

"My father came back and became furious with her. I did not know it all back then, but now I understand that she broke her word to him. She also got pregnant with another man's child. And my father never knew."

Sigurd glanced at the fjord, seeing his father and himself in a fishing boat. He remembered how Vigdis and he had run around the beach as children and gathered pebbles. He remembered longships with sails of different colors arriving. He used to hold his breath in anticipation of guests, stories, and merchandise from overseas.

All that was gone now. Because he'd trusted women.

"She gave birth to Vigdis and died in childbirth."

He turned to meet Donna's eyes. They were wide and full of emotion.

"My sister brought death to my people. My father died in that battle as did half of the men from our village. I was such a fool to have trusted her. All my fault, I sent her to Fuldarr. My father was right after all—women can't be trusted."

Sigurd turned towards the fjord. Despite his bitter words, he was surprised to find how good it felt to have poured out all the venom, like pus from a rotting wound. The secret of his sister's birth had eaten at him, corroding his faith and his trust.

Donna was so immobile, she might have been a statue,

her eyes watching but not seeing the fjord. It was as if she struggled with her own inner pain. The air itself was silent and still, and in that stillness, her voice sang a spell. "Saying that all women are mistrustful is like saying that all cats are black."

Sigurd chuckled. His heart felt light, and he had a new feeling of peace in his chest, as if his lungs could fully expand for the first time in years. Her warm hand grasped his forearm, shooting a bolt of fire through him. Gods, she had such an effect on his body. He wanted to take her right then and there, but this was not the time.

"You can start with trusting me," she said. "I am a woman."

Sigurd wished he could do that.

She had organized the womenfolk today like he could never have done. Even though he had growled and sent them away, he had later seen that all the work they'd done was good. The fortress had grown faster today than it had on the best day with only men. She did not have an agenda, did she? If the Norn had sent her, she must be here to help. Because the gods wanted him to succeed.

Besides that, she was an outlander. Something was so different about her... Yet it was as if some part of him had known her all his life. Maybe even beyond.

He needed to know.

He turned to her and brought her towards him, wrapping his arms around her. It felt right, like she belonged there. "Can I? Trust you?"

Her lips parted. She was as affected as he was. She nodded.

He swallowed. "Show me."

CHAPTER TEN

*S*igurd's words echoed in Donna's ears. He wanted her to show him—to prove—that he could trust her.

It was a test.

And he wanted her to make the first move.

Donna's pulse quickened. Even though Sigurd had just poured his heart out to her, he was not the only one in torment. He stirred her own demons, her own maxims of life.

Sigurd had been so hurt by the most important women in his life. Just like Donna and her mother had been hurt —by men.

Maybe Sigurd and Donna were not so different, after all.

She swallowed.

Running her hands up his tunic, she felt his hard muscles under her fingertips. Her breath accelerated, and his chest started to rise and fall quicker. The masculine scent of his body drove her crazy.

Her hands wrapped around the back of his neck—gosh, he was so tall—and she reached up to kiss him. Their lips touched gently, and a wave of desire went through her. The taste of his mouth made her want to jump on him, but she also wanted to show him tenderness. This strong man had just opened his deepest wounds to her. Wounds she was all too familiar with.

He answered with a gentleness that mirrored her own. His mouth pressed softly at first, but soon he urged the kiss deeper, and his hands glided up and down her back. Bliss spread through her skin. His tongue separated her lips to dip inside, stroking hers, sending her head in a carousel-like spin and making her forget that the world existed.

Her fingers ran through the silk of his hair. His arms engulfed her as she planted delicate kisses around his lips, his beard, his high cheekbones. Then down his neck, over the violent beat of his pulse, past the Thor's hammer pendant that seemed to be almost an integral part of him, and down his chest.

He did not let her continue, for now. His hands went under her buttocks and lifted her as if she weighed nothing. Her legs wrapped around his waist. "I want you just for my own," he growled and walked further down the coastline away from the village, towards the undergrowth that bordered the pebbled ground of the beach, behind the last of the beached longships.

He let her down near the shrubs, which shielded them from the village and created a cozy wall of sorts. It was only them, the fjord, the mountains and the sky.

She undid the ties of his fur cloak and let it fall onto the beach.

With their eyes still locked, she let his arms rise and pulled his tunic up, revealing his powerful body. Her heart beat faster, and she ran her fingers down his chest muscles, to his ripped stomach. As she approached the line of his trousers, he sucked in a breath. She began planting slow, feathery kisses on the trail her fingers had just taken, marveling at the beauty and strength of him. She worshiped his body, loving him with every touch.

His hands, buried in her hair, stiffened as her lips came close to the line of his trousers. She realized this must be new for him, to let her lead. He did not stop her this time, like he had last night. Her chest tightened till she almost ached.

"You are in good hands," she whispered against his navel, moving to kneel before him on the fallen cloak.

Surrounded by mountains that rose into the sky-like walls, with the mirror of the fjord, the thick woods—with the whole world going still and quiet—her words sounded like a spell, like a vow, and Sigurd's fingers relaxed ever so slightly. It was barely noticeable and yet it told Donna everything.

She undid his trousers and let them fall. His erection sprung free and glorious. She planted a kiss on his tip, and he moaned and started shaking.

She realized how much trust he was putting in her, and how fragile that thread was between them. This mighty Viking who could squeeze her to death, break her bones if he chose to, who was never separated from his ax and who commanded and protected dozens of people, trembled before her, showing her—and only her—his vulnerability.

His trust.

She planted another wet kiss on the tip of his erection, and another tremble went through him.

This was new for her, too. She had given blow jobs a couple of times but never enjoyed it, always feeling inferior and used.

But now, she felt the opposite—powerful and loving and giving, like a goddess—and a Viking trembled waiting for her next move, fully in her hands.

So strong and so fragile.

"You are the most magnificent man I've ever seen," she whispered and heard him catch a breath. Then she wrapped her lips around his tip, gently enveloping it in her mouth and welcoming it with her tongue.

He groaned, the hard muscles of his hips bulging under her fingers. His cock swelled and jerked slightly. She gently sucked, and he let out a growl. She took him in deeper and sucked a little harder, encouraged by his reaction. The sensation of his velvety skin gliding in her mouth and his hardness against her tongue heated up her veins like liquid fire.

"What are you doing to me," he grunted through his teeth.

She only moaned against him.

"Your mouth…" He started to thrust gently.

She took him deeper, started sucking faster and harder, drunk from the power she had over him and the pleasure she gave him.

"Ah, Freyja, oh gods…" he moaned. "I won't last long…"

Donna almost smiled against him. She wanted him to have everything, to show him that she was ready to give without wanting anything in return.

He stiffened. "If you don't want me to spill, you better stop now."

Donna only stroked his length with her tongue in response.

Sigurd panted now, grunting but holding his voice back. He accelerated his thrusts into her mouth. They became almost violent now, but she took everything he gave. And with a few final thrusts, his seed spilled against her throat, salty and primal. Her insides clenched at the feeling of his release.

"Donna," he moaned her name like a plea. She took everything in without flinching, every last drop of him precious and dear.

She pulled her head back too look at him and he fell to his

knees, holding on to her shoulders for support. His forehead fell to hers, and he panted.

Donna's body buzzed from unfulfilled desire, the intensity of the experience, and love that radiated from her heart.

Her Viking, this big and powerful man, in her hands. Right by her heart.

Sigurd raised his chin and met her eyes. His were still clouded but shone with softness—and also something new. Confidence, or maybe peace. He looked younger, as if he'd just woken up from a deep sleep.

The significance of what had just happened melted something in her chest. She'd passed the test. He'd begun trusting her, even if just a little bit.

And she knew that she needed to trust him in return.

CHAPTER ELEVEN

*D*onna's head lay on Sigurd's shoulder, her placid, soft body pressed against his side. And, despite himself, a feeling of peace spread through his muscles where their skin connected. He played with her golden hair.

What she had just done to him—what he had just allowed her to do—this must be how the gods felt in Asgard every day. Free, and high, and drunk. The moment when he'd opened up to her, as he'd never opened up to anyone else in the world, had been like jumping into the abyss.

And she'd caught him.

The night hid them well now in the darkness, but it wouldn't last longer than a couple of hours. Not that he planned to sleep much at all.

"I can't stand men like you," Donna said. Sigurd froze. Anger flushed through his body in a wave of heat, and he tried to calm himself. Had he heard her wrong?

"What did you say?"

"I fight men like you every day. Guys who like to put women in their place, who take away women's jobs or don't give them jobs only because they are women. Men who don't think women should play an important role, take charge or, God forbid, do something significant."

He had no idea what she was talking about. Surely, those men had a reason to disregard women. He did. His shoulders ached from tension. He shifted, to break contact with her and contradict her, but she did not notice and continued.

"But I am also afraid of men like you," her voice lowered to a whisper, and he frowned. Fear was no small thing to admit. "My mother raised me alone. She is a beautiful woman. Smart. She always wanted me to be independent, to think with my own mind so that no man would be able to break my spirit. Like hers."

Sigurd could not imagine anyone or anything being able to break Donna's spirit. Her eyes shone in the moonlight, watching the night in front of her.

"His name was Joseph, and he was my mother's only serious relationship. I was six years old. He used to lock me up in my bedroom at night so that I wouldn't bother my mother and him. I couldn't even go to the bathroom. I still remember him as that big, tall man with the stern face who always ordered my mother around and told me to go play in my room. He was a lawyer in the firm where she had worked. Same level, same experience. He got my mother's promotion only because he was a man and she was a woman. Then they fired her because she'd allegedly sexually harassed him. In reality, he just wanted to cover his backside because office romances were a no-go," Donna's voice shook. "She never could find work again in Manhattan. She had such a great career in front of her. If not for him, she'd have been named a partner long ago in some kick-ass firm."

Some of her words made no sense to Sigurd. But he understood that the man had done a similar thing to her mother that Vigdis had done to him and his father. Betrayal united Donna and him—across time and across distance.

"Some people plant rotten seeds in us, and we let them," Sigurd said. "Joseph did that to you."

Donna breathed out, tears welled in her eyes. She met his gaze. "And Vigdis—to you."

He nodded, bitterness coiling in his stomach.

Donna continued. "And Daniel did to me what Joseph did to my mother."

Sigurd's fists clenched. He did not know Daniel, but he was ready to cut his heart out and throw it to the crows. Donna was too, by the looks of her. With her golden hair, her body taut and her face burning with an emotion that resembled battle-fury, she could be a Valkyrie.

"He did not take my promotion or anything like that. But he did make me see a future with him and almost abandon everything I stood for—my independence, fighting for women's rights, and the law. Everything. And then he threw me away like a used napkin."

"Odin help me, the man would be long dead had I known him."

Donna let out a chuckle mixed with a sob and relaxed a little. "Yeah. There were times I wished that, too. Since then —well, since Joseph, but especially since Daniel—I just could not keep my cool if I had an opponent that reminded me of either of them. An alpha male." She quickly glanced at him and blushed. "Like you."

Silence hung heavy between them.

"Are you comparing me to those two piles of cow turds?"

Donna rose on her elbow. Her soft breast brushed against his skin, so full and delicious, sending desire through his body.

"I'm not! I mean, you are the same type of man. You command, and you expect everyone to jump at your every word, and you certainly discriminate against women."

Sigurd ground his teeth. "I have never betrayed a woman

67

in my life. If anything, I was too soft with Vigdis and protected my mother. And everything I do is to protect my people, even if I forbid women to do certain things. It's all for the better of the village. Do not dare to put me in the same boat as those two maggots."

Donna lay her hand on his chest, and a wave of tingles spread through the place where their skin touched. "I don't, Sigurd. Not anymore."

Not anymore. Sigurd's nostrils flared at the thought that she could ever have assumed anything like that about him before. But then again, he had accused her of things, too.

"Sigurd, I never told any of this to anyone. I don't even think I admitted it to myself."

The tension in Sigurd's stomach softened. He drew her to him. The connection between them, being here on the edge of the fjord, shielded by the mountains and witnessed by the sky, it was like the gods wanted them to come together. He wanted her. He needed her now. She'd poured her heart out to him, just as he had done, and he wanted to show her that the empty, raw space inside of her was safe.

He kissed her, his hands traveling down her back, which curved like the most beautiful longship. He rolled her onto her back and covered her with his body, still devouring her mouth. Liquid heat radiated from where their lips touched, soft brushes of her sleek tongue made him moan into her mouth.

But just as he was about to indulge in her breasts, gravel rustled next to him.

Sigurd drew himself up, his hand shooting to where his ax lay—but a booted foot stood on the long handle. Sigurd shielded Donna, who gasped. He hooked the man's ankle with one foot and kicked him under the knee with the other. The man fell back, and Sigurd pinned him to the ground, his ax pressed against the man's throat.

"Donna, stay back," he barked, then turned to the man. "Who are you?"

"Lord, I mean no harm. Your sister sent me."

"Harm and my sister always come together."

"She sent me with a message." The man's hand struggled to move under Sigurd, but he held him tight. "She gave me something for you… If you just let me take it out of my travel purse…"

"Do you take me for a fool? Do not move a finger."

Sigurd searched the man with one hand. As his fingers came across a sword, an ax and a scramasax, he removed each weapon and threw it far away. He found a purse and tossed it to Donna.

"See what is in there."

She was already dressed and caught the purse, her eyes wide. She began rummaging, removed a small leather pouch and opened it. She revealed a tiny wooden figure. "I think it's a fox."

"Let me see," Sigurd stretched out a hand, and Donna hurried to give the object to him. It was indeed a little carved wooden fox that used to be Vigdis's favorite toy. Sigurd had carved it for her. It had been her amulet of luck and well-being.

A dull ache ran through Sigurd's chest. "What is the message?"

"Fuldarr has almost gathered an army. He will attack soon. Very soon."

The blood left Sigurd's face and body. Already? They were not prepared. The fortress would not be built on time.

"Why should I trust you?"

"My name is Bjarni Bjarnison, lord. I am loyal to your sister. She was kind to me, and I swore to protect her." The man's voice deepened as he spoke, and Sigurd saw tenderness in his eyes. Did Bjarni love his sister? Did she love him? Sigurd frowned and studied the man.

Bjarni continued. "I saw them with my own eyes. Five dragonships came, all full of men."

Cold sweat dripped down Sigurd's spine. Five dragonships could contain between twenty and thirty dozen warriors. He only had fifty men.

They were doomed.

Vigdis's lover or not, the man could not be trusted. He still could be a spy. Sigurd grabbed the edge of the Bjarni's tunic and tore a long piece. He tied the man's hands behind him and bound his legs with another piece.

"Jarl, I am not lying. Odin knows, you should not mistreat the messenger who may have just saved you."

Sigurd tore another piece and put it into the man's mouth.

"Shut up. Let me think."

"Sigurd, you must—" Donna said.

"Let me think, Donna!"

She closed her mouth, a frown on her face. Odin help him, the man had either just brought news of sure death or was Fuldarr's spy.

How long did they have? Five dragonships was already an army. Was Fuldarr waiting for more, or was he already on his way? In either case, Sigurd's fifty men wouldn't stand a chance. With the current condition of the fortress, it would be a slaughter.

There was not a moment to waste. They'd need to double their efforts. Triple. Build even at night. Build now.

Sigurd started putting on his trousers in haste. He'd go wake up the men, and they'd start building again.

"Sigurd, what are you planning to do?" Donna said.

"Build the fortress, what else?" He removed the ties on Bjarni's ankles, grabbed him by the collar and yanked him up. He needed to lock the man up. "No spying around for you, Bjarnison."

The man mumbled something through the gag. Sigurd shoved him and went towards the great longhouse holding Bjarni by the upper arm. It was too bad the man might be a spy. Sigurd could use his him on the construction site.

"Sigurd, you have to let the women help," Donna said, hurrying after him.

Sigurd clenched his teeth. Something in him had shifted. He trusted Donna. But, although the women had done good work today, it was only a matter of time before they made mistakes. And those mistakes could kill them all. "Out of the question."

"Out of the question? Be reasonable! You won't make it without more workers."

"We will. We will build day and night, pause only when it's full dark. The boys will stop combat training and help build. The women can bring food. We'll sleep in shifts. We'll work faster."

"You are not serious! This plan is absolutely insane. You can't function like this for days."

"We will make a sacrifice to Odin and Tyr, the god of battle, and ask the gods for help."

Donna snorted. "The gods! Don't get me started. Even if the gods exist, where is the guarantee that they'll help you? You'll be exhausted by the time Fuldarr gets here. How will you fight?"

Sigurd clenched his teeth till his jawbones ached. The reminder of his confession brought heat to his face. She was right, he must have gone insane for a minute when something drove him to tell her about his biggest pain. Or maybe she'd cast some spell on him. He should not have done it. He needed to stay strong. Logical. The way he'd operated his whole life worked. Donna was a temporary distraction, a disruption, and she would be gone soon. "What do you know about our ways? You are an outsider."

Donna blinked, an expression of shock on her face. Her voice breaking she said, "After everything you just told me?"

Guilt stung him. He knew he must have hurt her, but he had to save his people. "Just stay out of this. No more tricks, no more women's riots. Bring me food and water to the construction site from time to time, like every woman whose man works on the fortress will. There's nothing more that you can do."

Donna's eyes blazed with fury in the darkness.

"Watch me." She turned and walked to the great hall without waiting for him.

CHAPTER TWELVE

*A*s Donna marched towards Asa's home, she fumed with anger. She could not believe him. Stubborn man! He had opened up to her, and she'd thought he'd changed, but at the first sign of trouble he'd reverted back to his default setting. And now he was pushing her away.

Fine.

If he thought she'd watch the men drive themselves to early graves and bring him food like an obedient little servant, he was an even bigger idiot than she'd thought.

Donna stopped before the door to Asa's longhouse. The faint smell of woodsmoke reached her nose. Unlike in many of the other houses, Asa's door had no gaps between the weathered planks. Floki had undoubtedly repaired them under Asa's supervision. Donna felt guilty to wake her up, but if Sigurd wanted to act now, so would she.

Donna decided against knocking, no need to wake the whole household. She opened the door—marveling that the Norsemen did not even bother locking their homes—and stepped into the house without a sound. The embers of the long hearth glowed in the darkness, barely illuminating the silhouettes lying on benches that ran along the walls. People wheezed in their sleep, a couple of men snored like engines.

Donna found Asa curled together with Floki in the furthest corner of the room. She touched the woman's shoulder, the linen of her shift warm under Donna's fingertips. Asa jerked up, and her hand shot under her pillow, probably for a weapon.

"Asa, it's Donna."

She froze, her eyes squinting from sleep. "What is it?"

"I need your help." Donna hesitated. Would she betray Sigurd if she told Asa the news of the attack? Everyone would know in a few hours anyway. And she needed to act. "Sigurd got a message from Vigdis. Fuldarr has gathered troops and is about to attack us."

Asa's hand covered her mouth. Floki sat up, his eyes wide, and Donna cursed herself for not asking Asa to go outside.

"Loki's turd," he whispered.

Donna nodded. "There's no time to waste, but Sigurd won't let the women help. We must build the fortress anyway."

Floki's face straightened. "Disobey the jarl, again? He will banish us from the village."

Donna swallowed. Was she right to ask this of them?

"Yes. But if we do as he says, there will be no village to be banished from."

Asa's mouth curved. Floki held Donna's gaze for a while, and she thought he'd contradict her again, but he said, "I will help you. You women need a foreman with experience. The jarl means well, but everyone can see that without more manpower we will all be dead."

Donna squeezed his hand in gratitude. Apparently, not every Viking was as stubborn as Sigurd.

Floki continued, "We'll build where the arch is. The jarl

does not plan to construct there yet. It is a small enough space for us to manage on our own."

The tension in Donna's muscles, which she had not noticed before, released. She said, "We'll just do it. Not in secret. But also not announcing it openly."

Asa and Floki both gave curt nods.

Asa woke a few women from her household and explained the plan to them. Outside, the sun was rising, and its first rays warmed Donna's cheeks. But the atmosphere in the village was somber, as if a cloud of fear cast dark shadows over everything. Together with Donna, they visited the women Asa trusted. Sigurd had already woken up many people—men had their quick breakfasts and walked to the construction sites, their faces stern, worry deep in their eyes.

They gathered a dozen women. Five more went to cut down trees in the forest. They started slowly, but after they got into the rhythm of cutting the logs, removing the branches, sharpening the edges and planting the stakes in the trench, the work went faster. The women started singing, altogether, a song that told the story of Brunhild, the legendary shield-maiden. The melody sounded primal and ancient, and after a while, Donna joined in, humming because she did not know the words. Floki's voice droned in the background. Their song created a space, an invisible dome under which they were united, working as one. Donna had never felt this kind of connection in her own time and only wished Sigurd was here with them, singing.

To Donna's astonishment, they'd already finished the palisade when night started to descend. It stood from both sides, attached to the rocks of the arch, and they were hanging the gate on hinges. Donna stood back to admire the work they had done together. Her muscles buzzed from exhaustion, her eyelids heavy. There was only one thing to do—fix the fallen rock of the stone arch itself.

Once the arch was whole again, would she really be able to go back anytime she wanted? The prospect of leaving Sigurd made Donna's feet drag.

Floki and one of the taller women lifted Donna up on their shoulders so that she could fix the rock. Her hands shook—surely from exhaustion, she told herself. The stone fit as though it never had separated from the arch, and stayed as if glued. There weren't even any cracks.

As the arch became whole, a feeling overcame Donna. She knew, just as she knew that the sun would rise tomorrow, that the arch was alive...and magical...and it would swallow her. She could feel it just like she could feel her own heartbeat.

Donna's fingers dug into the shoulders on which she sat. Her skin prickled as if a net of razor blades covered her. Something sucked all breath from her lungs. "Put me down," she whispered.

When her feet hit on the ground, she fell as if cut, and crawled as far away from the arch as possible. Arms embraced her from behind, and a feeling of safety wrapped around her like a warm shawl. "Shhh, you are safe," Sigurd whispered in her ear, and she relaxed. "I won't let you go yet."

Donna breathed easier, the warmth of his arms around her calming her down. She slowly turned her head to look at him. His handsome face hung over her, their eyes locked, and everything else ceased to exist. He looked at her with concern.

"Are you mad?" Donna said.

Sigurd's expression turned to one of lustful longing. He brushed her upper arm with his fingers, and Donna's stomach fluttered. But then he broke eye contact and glared at the palisade, looking torn between relief and anger. He rose, and Donna stood up as well, her feet steadier now. Sigurd walked towards the newly constructed wall.

"All of you," he growled. "You disobeyed the orders of your jarl. You knew there would be consequences."

Donna's skin chilled. Was he about to punish them?

Sigurd stood right by the palisade and inspected it closely, his hand brushing along the wall. He opened and closed the gate and glanced up at the stone arch. His head turned to Floki.

"And you, Floki, you helped—"

"Jarl," Floki interrupted, "I disagree. The women should help. I supervised them, and I tell you, there is no fault in this palisade. It will stand and protect. The work here is done—only thing left is to bar the gate."

Sigurd's mouth curved down in anger. "If we were not under the greatest threat to our existence, I would have you all banished from the village." He scowled at Donna. "Let me guess, you initiated this?"

Donna's chin rose. "Yes. If you need to punish someone, punish me." An unwanted thrill went through Donna at the thought of how he might do that, but she chased it away. "We will continue building, though, whether you want it or not. Just look." She gestured towards the palisade. "Is this not helpful? Did it not make you feel a little easier to see this part of the fortress finished?"

Sigurd crossed his arms on his chest and opened his mouth to speak when a shout made their heads turn.

"Jarl!" A boy not older than twelve ran on the path. "Hurry! There's been an accident."

Sigurd's face lost its color, and he ran after the boy. Donna and the rest followed him. It was now almost dark. The indigo sky glowed with gold behind the mountains to the west. When they arrived at the construction site by the beach, some men still worked, but a dozen or so stood in a circle leaning over someone.

Sigurd was already kneeling beside the figure, and as

Donna came closer, she saw a man lying on the ground and clawing at his leg. His ankle was twisted in an unnatural way, and Donna felt sick.

One of the men explained, "We set the stake in the wrong place because of the darkness, and it fell. Normally, we would have held it, but honestly, lord, we don't have much strength left."

Asa leaned over the man. "I can set the bone, but—"

"But what?" Sigurd growled.

She shot him a quick glance. "Injuries like this… I don't know if the bone will heal properly."

Sigurd froze, his face an expressionless mask. "Will he be a cripple?"

Donna shut her eyes, fear slipping down her spine like an icicle.

Asa looked at the broken ankle from different angles. "I don't know yet."

"But he might be?"

"He might."

Donna's hand automatically landed on Sigurd's shoulder. The guilt was probably killing him.

She glanced back at the palisade. Fires illuminated small parts of it, but it was mostly dark, and Donna wondered how the men could do any work at all. The fortress had advanced since Donna had seen it last night, but looking at what remained to be built, the progress seemed heartbreakingly slow. Knocks of hammers and sharp shouts of commands and insults filled the air. But the insults did not sound like friendly men's banter. They were full of spite. This was so different from the arch construction site, when the women and Floki had sung in unison.

Asa asked the men to carry the injured man in her house and went with them. Sigurd followed them with a haunted look on his face, then turned back to the men. "Stop the construction!" he roared. "Go home, rest. Come back tomorrow as agreed with the first light."

The men laid whatever they were holding on the ground, got down from the towers and walked back home with tired looks on their faces.

Sigurd stood silent and immobile, his hands propped on his hips, studying the ground.

"Sigurd—" Donna said as softly as she could, but he interrupted her.

"I know. Allow the women to build."

He met her gaze, and his face was distorted with an inner struggle. Oh, her brave, lovely, strong warrior. The injury to that man must be torturing him. He could have stopped the work sooner. He could have already employed the women's help. And while it was all true, Donna didn't blame him. And she hoped he wouldn't blame himself, although she was certain he would.

"I will," he said, his voice cracking. Relief flooded Donna's body. She rushed to him and hugged him. His arms engulfed her and pressed her tight to him. Warmth spread through her chest as if he'd just lit a candle in the middle of her heart.

And for the first time since she'd arrived, hope bloomed in Donna.

CHAPTER THIRTEEN

*O*din pierce him with his spear, Donna was right.

The combined forces of everyone in the village allowed them to make progress like never before. After just a week, the palisade at the beachfront rose, and the scent of hewn wood enveloped the village. They left a gap for a gate in the middle. The first defensive tower had been finished completely. The second one was well underway, and the third one just started. Southern wind brought the scent of the sea, and with it, the reminder of Fuldarr's threat.

Working together as a team with a woman made Sigurd feel strangely balanced. He was starting to get used to her. Seeing her so close during the day, as she mixed clay or carried logs with other women, spread the sensation of peace in his core. He caught himself many times admiring the way her breasts bounced ever so slightly under the fabric of her dress as she walked. The way her hips swayed. He was looking forward to the short nights, when she gave herself so eagerly to him, and her body sang in his arms.

The Norn was a good matchmaker. Had Donna been born in his age, he'd turn the world upside down to marry her and make her his forever. She was the most beautiful creature he had ever seen. Smart, willful, and outspoken, she was a worthy wife to a jarl.

This must have been how Freyr, the god of sun and fertility, felt when he first laid eyes on the beautiful Gerðr and was ready to give up his invincible sword to marry her.

Sigurd was ready to sacrifice such a sword, too, had he possessed one.

Yet the decision to give up something was not his.

It was hers.

And the odds were not in Sigurd's favor.

He chased the thoughts away like a horde of rodents. He avoided even looking in the direction of the finished arch and immersed himself in work. As the days had gone by, he'd begun to notice that a group of men openly disapproved of the women working by their sides. Sigurd himself was not quite at peace with the solution, but the work was done, and it was done well.

Mostly.

By the end of the first week, the group at the beachfront site steamed with anger. Geirr, the biggest opponent, bossed the women around and scolded them if they did something amiss, or if a woman had to pause to take a breath.

That morning, the towers boiled with activity as workers continued construction. Then Sigurd heard arguing, and his gut clenched as he saw Donna's figure right in the middle of a small gathering of people who gesticulated and talked in heated tones.

"What is this?" Sigurd barked as he approached them.

Donna's head shot to him. Relief relaxed her features, and he breathed easier. "Sigurd, thank God you're here. You must stop this nonsense."

"Women should not be allowed to do skilled work, jarl!" Geirr interrupted. "Brama came up the tower, took my hammer and started nailing the planks together while I was away for a minute—"

"And what did you do, Geirr?" Brama, a younger woman, held her left shoulder with her right hand. "He pushed me away, jarl, and I fell down the ramp."

"I did not mean for her to fall! Who told her to do anything on the tower?"

Sigurd's nostrils flared. A female should not do work that required construction skill, but harming a woman was shameful for a man.

Before he could say anything, his beautiful maiden of justice spoke again: "You know what, that's it. This is not the first time the women have been shoved, pushed, and threatened on this construction. I think it's time for you ladies to learn to defend yourselves against that and any threats to come." She eyed Geirr up and down. "Especially if someone assumes they have the right to touch you."

Geirr bared his teeth, and Sigurd's fists clenched. He made a step towards the man, but Donna continued, and everyone's attention was drawn back to her. "The enemy is coming. Wouldn't it be sensible for the women to know how to protect themselves?"

The women nodded. Sigurd watched her full lips moving and could not believe his ears. Women fighting? Simple women, not shield-maidens? Loki must have clouded Donna's mind.

"There will be none of that."

Donna glared at him, her cheeks starting to redden. "It makes sense, Sigurd. The fortress is progressing well. Instead of watching such idiots as Geirr picking fights with the women, allow at least some of them to learn self-defense. If we helped with the construction, we might help with the fighting."

Geirr laughed. "Jarl, am I hearing her right? I might have seaweed in my ears—"

Sigurd's hand rose to shut him up. "Not a word more, Geirr." He turned to Donna and to the women who watched him with frowns. "Combat is brutal. Axes, swords, and shields. Gore, broken bones, and spilled guts. Rare women learn to fight well and become shield-maidens. But combat needs lengthy training. Time we don't have."

"They could at least learn the basics to protect against rape." Donna glanced sideways at Geirr, and he glared at her.

"Elbows and knees will do nothing against a warrior armed with steel and burning for a woman."

Donna pursed her lips and crossed her arms over her chest, making the fabric stretch and hug her breasts. The urge to touch her sent a bolt of heat through Sigurd's groin. Loki's mischief. How could he still react to her like that, in the middle of a construction site?

Sigurd gritted his teeth and looked at the people around him.

"Self-defense will do nothing for you," he said. "When the enemy comes, and the women are fighting on the battlefield, the warriors will have to split their attention to protect them and fight their own battle at the same time. We'll lose."

He did not believe what he was about to say. His men would protest. The women might think a spirit had taken over his body. "But there's still something the women can do to protect the village from a distance. Archery."

Donna's eyes brightened. "Yes! Brilliant, Sigurd." She gripped his hand with both of hers, sending a pleasant buzzing through his skin. Seeing her approval, her happiness, made warmth radiate throughout his body and his heart drum in his chest. He wanted to make her feel like that every day of her life.

If they survived.

He continued, "It does not mean that you will be out of danger. Enemy archers will aim at you, too. But you will be in the watchtowers."

The women did not seem to be frightened. They watched him with something that resembled pride, and his own chest thrust out slightly with pride for his women. Asa spoke, and he knew she expressed the voices of many.

"Jarl, you should have asked us long ago."

Sigurd nodded. "Halfdan is the best archer. He'll teach you. Gather by the stone arch." Stone arch… His eyes shot to Donna's and he immediately glanced somewhere else. Anywhere else. "It's far enough away so that you don't hurt anyone while you train."

Geirr made a step towards Sigurd. "Jarl, is this wise?"

"It is, Geirr. It is wise to do anything to protect you and your family and everyone in this village."

Donna raised her chin. "I will learn, too."

The muscles of Sigurd's stomach quivered. His pulse sped. "Not you."

"You can't tell me what to do—"

Sigurd felt the eyes of his people on him. He gripped Donna's elbow and led her away.

"Do not dare undermine my authority in front of my people," he growled.

"But—"

"There will be no archery training for you."

They stood now behind a building, shielded from prying eyes, and he wrapped his arms around her—something he itched to do the whole day long. The feeling of being home enveloped him. "I can't risk your life."

"And I can't just stand by and watch everyone else die."

He planted a kiss on her lips, and their softness kindled a fire in his groin. "Have you ever been in a battle?"

She blushed. "No."

"Have you ever seen death?"

"No."

"Then you have no idea what awaits you."

Donna paled a little, her skin almost translucent. Then stubbornness hardened her eyes, and they became as blue as the deep sea in summer. "You're right. I have no clue. But, Sigurd, I am going to learn to shoot a bow with the women of your village. And if you think you can stop me, you don't have the slightest idea who I am. And if that's the case, maybe it's better we stop this…whatever it is between us."

Sigurd swallowed, and panic shot through him like a lightning bolt. He did not want to end this, especially not now as she melted in his arms, soft and delicious.

But Donna was right. He knew she was a warrior at heart. Seeing her risk her life made him want to cut his own heart out, just to shield her from harm. But even worse would be to have her completely unprepared and see her killed because of his mistrust.

He had to trust her to learn to fight and protect herself as he trusted his warriors.

"I do know you, Donna. I knew you from the moment I saw you. Through time, through the hundreds of years. You are a shield-maiden, your weapons are words and arguments, but it is time you learn to fight with steel and wood."

CHAPTER FOURTEEN

A week later

THE ROAR of a war horn cut through the air as Donna and Sigurd ate breakfast at the long table, their arms and hips pressed against each other like schoolchildren's.

Since Donna had begun archery training, they no longer saw each other for most of the day, but their nights were full of fire. When they were apart, Donna felt as if a weight pressed on her lungs. Once back in Sigurd's bedchamber, she could breath again. They were drawn together like waves to the shore, and held each other close until first light, when it was time to go their separate ways.

They did not speak much, just whispered against each other's skin as they made love.

And once or twice, when he was deep inside of her, bringing her to ever-greater levels of ecstasy, Donna caught the "I love you" that almost escaped her mouth like a prisoner longing for freedom. It was born somewhere in her chest and rose up her throat like a bubble, only to be stopped by her gritted teeth.

How would she ever leave? How would she live without him?

The horn continued to sing its heart-gripping song as Sigurd's and Donna's eyes locked.

Death came knocking. Fear chilled Donna to the bone. She'd give everything to see Sigurd unharmed.

"Don't you dare die." Her lips barely moved, as hard as wood.

Tears welled in her eyes, but she forbade them to spill. Sigurd cupped the back of her neck and planted a kiss on her mouth. It had the aftertaste of goodbye, cutting Donna's stomach like a million knives.

Sigurd stood up, took his ax, which lay next to him on the bench, and shouted, "The enemy is here! To your places!"

He called one of the teenage boys to help him put on his war gear, and they went to the bedchamber. Donna followed him there to take her bow and arrows, and Sigurd told her to put on his leather armor while he put on his brynja, which shone with thin iron chains and must have been as heavy as half a car.

Then they rushed together towards the watchtowers hand in hand. Men were already fully armored, and women archers stood in position.

The fortress was still not finished. The beachfront palisade had a gap on the right side, where Donna and Sigurd had made love two weeks ago. The eastern side was also still under construction, but Fuldarr didn't know that. The only completed site was the stone arch. Two watchtowers stood solid. The third had only the supporting pillars and was, therefore, useless. Under Thorsten's guidance, villagers were quickly piling earth up by the gap, planting long spikes into it at an angle. Female archers were already waiting there together with two dozen fully armored warriors.

The gate was still open, and the sight through it stopped Donna's heart. Eight longships slid towards them at full speed, oars rising and falling. Five or so ships had bright red-and-blue sails, but the rest had different ones: green, and yellow, and plain white.

"He found allies," Sigurd spat out the words. "Vigdis did not lie."

Donna thought about the violence and the deaths that those ships would bring. She had to try a peaceful way. "Sigurd, let me go negotiate. It's what I do for living. I can—"

"You are out of your mind if you think I'll let you do that. You are no one to Fuldarr and have no negotiation power. What is to stop him from killing you on sight or taking you prisoner?"

Donna clenched her fists. She was afraid for him, and she could not sit and wait for him to be killed. "Let's go together then. I will be useful. I am from the future, remember? I know tricks. Maybe we can resolve this peacefully so that no one has to die."

Sigurd bared his teeth and looked up at the approaching ships from under his eyebrows. "There's more chance that Loki will stop plotting. No, Donna, there won't be peace today. Blood will spill—Fuldarr's blood." He touched the Thor's hammer pendant around his neck, seeking the god's protection. "But you are right. We can win some time for the people to do last-minute preparations. Get your tricks ready, maiden of justice."

Sigurd took Floki and five of his strongest warriors to accompany Donna and him, and they stood on the beach waiting for the ships to arrive.

Donna's knees shook as the ships approached. Her heart tap-danced, and sweat broke out on her skin in a sticky film.

Fear melted her bones. She had never been so scared in her entire life. They said New York was dangerous. New York was a piece of cake compared to this. Real war came at her like a train at full speed. And she could not do anything to stop it.

She could only run. Yes, that was an option. Run, right now, to the arch and disappear in time, back to the safety and the warmth of the twenty-first century.

But she would be damned if she did that. Because the man her heart beat for stood by her side. The bravest, the strongest, the dearest man who had her—body and soul. And she must be brave and strong for him. Someone he could rely on —him and his people. Donna's chin rose and she gripped the bow till her nails dug into her flesh.

The first ships arrived, and for a moment, no one spoke. Warriors on the boats had already built a shieldwall.

"Fuldarr, show yourself!" Sigurd yelled. "Let's talk."

A tall man with long, straight black hair appeared. Something about him reminded her of that night in her Manhattan bedroom, of Joseph, who had gone through her mom and Donna's life like a tornado, leaving them broken and empty, and never the same. Her chest tightened and her mind went hazy.

"What do you possibly want to talk about, Sigurd? I am about to finish what I had started last year."

He gestured, and a woman appeared behind him. She was pale and thin, her shiny blond hair gathered up in an elaborate style. This must be Vigdis.

"Maybe you want to see your sister? All right then. Let's go down, wife." He jumped down into the water, and several warriors followed him. One pushed Vigdis to do the same.

When Fuldarr's party stopped ten feet or so from them, Donna understood why Fuldarr wanted to come down with Vigdis. He wanted Sigurd to see her in every detail. A classic move to push the opponent's buttons and make him emotional. Donna's feet turned to ice as she saw Vigdis's face. One eyelid was purple and so swollen that it completely shut the eye. Caked blood covered an eyebrow, a bruise bloomed on her cheek, and a cut split her lower lip. Donna glanced at Sigurd. His face looked as if it was carved from stone, which meant that he was beyond anger. She shifted towards him and straightened her back. If he was about to lose his mind, she should be the one keeping a clear head.

"What did you do to my sister?" Sigurd growled.

"That's between my wife and me. Rest assured, she deserved it. You are not the only one she betrayed. It seems she can't help herself."

Donna saw from the corner of her eye how Sigurd's hand started to shake, and the bones of his hand tensed so much from the strength with which he gripped the handle of the ax, she feared they'd rip through his skin.

She had to intervene, or Sigurd would explode. "What will it take for you to leave peacefully?" she asked.

Fuldarr's eyes darted to her and he cocked his head. "And who is she, Sigurd? New wife?"

Donna felt Vigdis's eyes on her and blushed, catching herself on the desire for Sigurd's only family to like her. How silly.

"She is not my wife."

This was true, but it stung Donna a little.

"Then why should I talk to you, woman?"

Sigurd was about to say something, but Donna intervened. "Because I am from the future."

All eyes fell on her. Fuldarr's body stiffened and he stared at her. "What?"

"A Norn sent me here from more than a thousand years in the future."

"Donna!" Sigurd's voice slapped her.

But she was too far into the plan. She wanted to scare Fuldarr, to intimidate him, to make *him* unsure and emotional.

"And I already told Sigurd all the secrets and technologies and innovations that he needs to know."

Judging from Fuldarr's body language, it was working. His brows knit together, eyes widened in surprise and—yes, small, barely noticeable—fear.

She pressed. "And behind that palisade, there are machines that spit fire and warriors made of iron that fight on their own."

"You are lying," Fuldarr growled, but his voice lost its confidence. "You are just a wench."

"I am telling the truth—"

"Donna, stop!" Sigurd snapped.

Fuldarr's eyes flicked between them and a slow sneer widened his lips. "What's wrong, Sigurd? Last year you sent me your sister. Now you are hiding behind another woman's skirt. Where did you lose your balls?"

Donna's breath caught. She had not lived with the Vikings long, but she'd already learned that the worst insult to a Viking was to offend his masculinity. Sigurd had already been shaken. Now, he was about to explode. The reminder about his mistake with Vigdis, and what that had cost his family, was too much.

His face was twitching, his mouth distorted in a snarl, and his feet trembled ever slightly, ready to launch himself at Fuldarr.

And die.

Fuldarr saw it, too. A barely noticeable smile stretched his lips, and he lifted one arm, about to signal his warriors. Vigdis's face froze in desperation. Sigurd's warriors took their positions, too.

Donna had no time to spare, and just before the crazy

Vikings clashed in a massacre, she threw her bow to the ground and stepped towards Fuldarr. "Wait!"

Everyone froze, their eyes on her. Good. A surprise. This would shake Sigurd's bloodthirst. "Fuldarr, let Sigurd and his men go back to the fortress. If you do, I will give myself to you. I will tell you all the secrets from the future."

She did not want to see Sigurd's face. She could not. The pain he must have felt, of another woman betraying him like that, after he had trusted her with his biggest pain, after he had changed for her, after he had started listening to her advice.

She must have just stabbed him in the heart.

But better this than have him and the whole village slaughtered.

Fuldarr's eyes shot to Sigurd, and from the triumph on their enemy's face, Donna did not need to see her man to know that the hurt was written all over him. Fuldarr nodded, and with a sinking heart, Donna ran towards him and stood by his side, between him and Vigdis. When she turned to face Sigurd, blood froze in her veins.

He looked as if someone had just stabbed him in the gut, but he still stood in position ready to launch himself at Fuldarr. She had to do something.

"I am just joining the winning team."

Sigurd's eyes widened, and his face reddened as if she was strangling him. Tears blurred Donna's vision. "Fuldarr, I never met a man with such a great army, even back in my time," she said, her voice trembling. She hated herself. But it was working. Fuldarr's chest puffed with pride, he believed she was on his side.

So did Sigurd.

His face hardened, and without saying another word, he turned and strode away, his head high, as if Donna did not exist.

CHAPTER FIFTEEN

"*A*rchers, ready!" Sigurd yelled as the gates of the fortress closed with a thump behind him. He climbed the ramp of one of the watchtowers. The women stood, already in position, and drew their bows. "Shoot!" The first storm of arrows poured down on the enemy.

He commanded his mind not to think about what Donna had just done—not now—but the memory sank its claws into him. His chest throbbed from inside as if it was being minced into dinner meat. Across the beach, Donna stood where he had left her. He could feel her eyes on him even from a distance. Fuldarr gesticulated, sending the warriors running towards the fortress. They spilled from the ships like grain from sacks and formed shieldwalls.

Odin, do not let our arrows touch those two women.

Everything about what Donna had just done rang of betrayal. Betrayal seemed to grow on that beach like moss. Vigdis's. Donna's. Same place. Same enemy. The thought ground his insides into dust.

The enemy began shooting arrows at them, too. Women around him ducked under their shields, and arrows thunked against the wood and the tower. But Sigurd stood as if nothing was happening around him.

Donna's eyes locked with his across the field of the enemy, across the wall. Across time.

And now she was in danger.

The woman who had betrayed him.

Sigurd roared.

Fury rose in him from his toes up like a cleansing fire. He'd fight, oh Odin, he'd fight. For his father. For his people. For the woman he loved.

Sigurd had to go where his people were most vulnerable —the unfinished part of the fortress. He hurried down the ramp.

"Odin!" Sigurd yelled as he reached the hill of piled-up earth spikes, many of which had enemy warriors planted on them. But they kept coming, and Sigurd immersed himself in the battle. "Odin!" he called again as he hacked into his first kill of the battle.

Arrows flew—theirs and the enemy's—and found their targets, splitting muscle and bone. People screamed, got wounded, and died. The enemy's shieldwalls grew thinner as the women's arrows found flesh, and gratitude spilled through Sigurd like warm mead at the thought that without the women's help, they all would have been slaughtered by now. Without Donna's help.

The thinned rows of the enemy reached the palisade and began their attempts to hop over the wall. Arrows took many warriors, but some landed on the other side, meeting Sigurd's men's swords and axes.

Steel clashed, wood split, bones broke, flesh tore. The fortress stood. Most of the enemy's men who breached the fortress died, but after a time, Sigurd's men started dying, too. Fuldarr simply had too many men.

And Donna did not stand a chance. She was in the enemy's power.

In the fury of the battle, everything came down to the essence of things—stab or run, duck or linger, live or die. And something became clear to Sigurd. Donna did not have a reason to go to Fuldarr as Vigdis had. She wanted to go back to her own time, and now she was further away from her goal than ever.

She'd put herself in more danger than she could imagine.

No, she did not betray.

She sacrificed herself. She did it for him. For his people.

There was just one thing to do.

If he killed Fuldarr, everything would stop. No harm would come to Donna or any more of his people.

He needed his best warriors. They'd make a break towards Fuldarr. And if they used the western gate—the arch, which, as far as he knew, was free—and went from the side, unnoticed, they'd have a chance.

Sigurd found Floki and five others, explained the plan, and they ran towards the arch. They went through the gate quietly, and then through the woods towards the rocky western side of the fjord where ships could not dock and the enemy would not know what lay beyond the woods.

When Sigurd and his men walked out of the forest onto the beach, they first trotted without shielding themselves, so that they would not appear suspicious and the enemy would not recognize them from a distance. Most of Fuldarr's men fought by the fortress, and only a handful stood behind. As they came close enough, Sigurd and his warriors began slicing their way towards Fuldarr, whose full attention was on the fortress.

It was a hard fight; there were twice as many of enemy as there were of them. After a while, Floki screamed and fell, a sword in his chest. Sigurd growled, the pain of losing his battle brother igniting his muscles into a frenzy of revenge. He cut and stabbed and split his way towards Fuldarr. But soon he saw the rest of his warband all lying on the ground.

It was Sigurd now against Fuldarr—and his army. Donna and Vigdis still stood by his side, their eyes round with horror.

Sigurd just had to do that last thing. He was so close. He launched himself on Fuldarr, disregarding the other warriors. They moved towards him, but Fuldarr stopped them with a raised hand.

He drew his sword, and Sigurd's ax clashed against it. Fuldarr's face, full of spite, flashed over him. Sigurd's muscles screamed and the breath caught in his throat. The hours of battle had exhausted him and planted a dull ache in his body, whereas Fuldarr had only just begun. Odin, give me strength, he thought, and gathering the remains of his power, pushed Fuldarr back and came at him, ax flashing. Sigurd grunted with every strike, the ax rang against the sword like a blacksmith's hammer.

But Sigurd had overestimated himself. His arms buzzed with exhaustion, and he took longer to strike each blow. Fuldarr used his hesitation to pick up the shield and raise it. Sigurd's ax stuck in the wood, and Fuldarr thrust his sword into Sigurd's side. His body exploded in pain, and he fell on one knee, but his father's brynja did not let the sword through.

With his ax gone, he drew his scramasax. The long and deadly dagger was a weak weapon against Fuldarr's long sword and the shield, but it was all he had. He called the last of his strength out of every inch of his body—and soul— and slashed low, aiming for Fuldarr's thigh. But his blade only cut through the air. Fuldarr's sword came at him, aiming for his shoulder, but Sigurd raised his weapon to block the sword, which met the scramasax and stayed on it.

Fuldarr pressed down on Sigurd, who had to put the pommel of the scramasax against his other palm to protect his neck. His blade opened the flesh of his hand, cutting him.

Sigurd's hands shook as Fuldarr's sword pushed the scramasax closer and closer to his neck. Sigurd roared and thrust up against him, but Fuldarr only pushed harder, his eyes bulging with the triumph of imminent victory.

The blade came closer and closer to Sigurd's neck. Fury and desperation boiled in him, but he did not have much strength left. He did not want to die. If he died, the whole village would. And what would happen to Donna and Vigdis? But he was losing, he knew it deep down in his bones. *Not like this, Odin.*

Then a female screeched somewhere behind Fuldarr, there was a *thump*, and the pressure on the blade released. Fuldarr's leg gave way, and he fell on the other knee. With the last of his strength, Sigurd thrust his scramasax deep into the man's eye.

Fuldarr screamed, his sword and shield dropped, and his hands clenched the blade. But life left him, and he fell sideways, blood staining the pebbles.

Behind him stood Vigdis. She panted and stared at Fuldarr's body, as if she could not quite believe what she had just done, her eyes wide. Her face grimaced in a mask of hatred, and she spat on him. Then she locked eyes with Sigurd and fell to her knees, tears streaming.

Donna ran towards him. He scooped her into his arms, his heartbeat loud in his eardrums. Her face wet with tears, she pressed her cheek to his gore-smudged face.

"Thank God, you're alive," she kept whispering in his ear.

The realization of victory finally hit him. His lungs still gulped for air, but he pumped his fist and roared. Fuldarr's warriors were already clambering back onto the ships. But the battle on the fortress continued, as people did not know what had happened on the beach.

"I killed your jarl," Sigurd roared like a warhorn. "You have no jarl!"

"Stop the fight!" Vigdis cried. "Stop!"

Sigurd glanced at her in surprise. She was the jarl now, as the widow, and she could have commanded her warriors to continue the battle. But Sigurd doubted she had much power over them. He doubted they'd risk their lives for her.

As Vigdis met his gaze, fear like he'd never seen before distorted her face. She stood up, no doubt to run towards one of the ships, and Sigurd launched himself at her, locking his arm around her neck. Donna shrieked.

"Not this time, Vigdis," he whispered in her ear. "Gods know, all of this is because of you, and you need to be punished for your betrayal."

She sobbed, "Please, Sigurd, I tried to help—"

He shook her and put his bloody hand on her mouth, "Shut up. Donna, give me my scramasax."

She nodded, her face torn between worry and relief. Once she did, he put the blade at Vigdis's neck so that her warriors would not decide to fight for her.

They didn't.

Fuldarr's army began to retreat. The beach filled with the rustle of the pebbles under their shoes. Men threw somber glances at Sigurd and kept climbing into the ships. "I guess they do not want to fight for the jarl who uses betrayal like a morning wash," he whispered in Vigdis's ear, and she closed her eyes, sobbing.

The dead and the wounded lay on the ground, and there were bodies along the waterline where Sigurd and his six warriors had cut their way towards Fuldarr, his battle brothers among them. Piles of corpses lay at the bottom of the fortress wall. The coppery scent of blood filled the air.

Sigurd felt Donna's hand on his forearm, and a wave of warmth and comfort went through him at her touch. He planted a kiss on her forehead, the presence of her, alive and well, replenishing his body with life—like a magic potion.

He'd won.

No one spoke a word, only the wounded moaned in pain. And as the last of the enemy's men left the beach, the breeze from the fjord brought whispers of the waves splashing against the longships, and Sigurd wondered if he heard the wings of Valkyries who came to gather the best warriors for Valhöll.

CHAPTER SIXTEEN

Sigurd stirred in bed. He felt Donna's gaze as if she stroked him with fur. He opened one eye. "Enough. I can feel your eyes on me."

Gods, she was the most beautiful thing he had ever seen, even right after waking up, even with puffy eyes and messy hair. But a shadow deep in her eyes stirred the dark worm of worry in his gut. The only thing that could shadow their happiness now, after the enemy was defeated, and after the fortress stood.

There was nothing more that would stop her from going home.

Not yet, gods, not yet.

He only knew one way to make her forget. He pulled her onto his chest, and the brush of her bare breasts against his skin sent scorching heat through his groin. His mouth took hers, craving her as a thirsty man craves water during a drought. He engulfed her, his hands digging into her smooth flesh, desperate.

She did not protest. She responded with the same desperation, devouring his mouth as if for the last time.

Something wet stroked his cheek, and he tasted salt on his tongue.

Sigurd spun her around and pinned her in the furs beneath him. She was crying.

"Did I hurt you?"

She shook her head and kissed him, pulling him to her.

No, he had not hurt her.

She was leaving him today.

He knew it like he knew his name. He felt it like he could feel her body under him.

No!

He needed to make her change her mind. The silk of her skin under his hands sent a tremor of desire through him. He stroked the fullness of her ripe breasts, as if they were treasure. She moaned and arched her back, and he continued down the softness of her belly, and then lower to the triangle of curls. His fingers brushed her there, and he followed them with soft, wet kisses. She arched her head back, moans of pleasure escaping her throat.

Yes, he'd make her forget all about New York.

At least for now.

His fingers stroked between the lips of her sex, sliding into the sleek warmth. Finding the sweetest spot, he circled lightly with his finger, pressing just enough to make Donna's nails dig into his shoulders and a whimper escape her lips.

He leaned down, his mouth melding with her sex, his tongue lashing the sweetest spot of her. Her taste, her smell, made his head spin and his erection stiffen even more. Filled him with the urge to plunge deep into her and make her tighten around him.

To feel that she was his.

He wanted to bring her the most pleasure she'd ever had, something that would bind her to him, and win the battle against time. His soul ached at the thought of losing her, and he continued his game until she begged, "Please Sigurd, oh please…I need you inside of me."

Her words tasted like honey, but he wanted to see how far he could take her. "Not yet," he murmured, and she groaned.

He worshiped her until she moaned just like every time right before she came, and he withdrew. Donna moaned in frustration. He stretched alongside her, his skin singing against hers, his hands caressing her breasts, his mouth teasing her ear.

"Sigurd, please," she turned to him, rubbing herself against him.

"Not yet."

His hands searched for the places that would make her shake with bliss. Her fingers glided against his skin down his stomach to his erection, and he sucked in his breath when they brushed against his length. He was not far from exploding, and it took all his willpower not to spread her thighs and sink into her warmth.

Instead, he returned to his previous position and resumed torturing her with his tongue. And, once again, when he felt her sex tighten and heard *those* moans, he withdrew.

After a few moments, he lay on his back and pulled her up on top of him. He loved seeing her ride him. Donna breathed heavily and wiggled against him. "Please, Sigurd."

That was it.

He lifted her up and drove into her. It felt like coming back home after a long and successful raid. She moaned and began moving on him, and he sank into the ocean of pleasure with every thrust, filling every small part of himself, every hair on his body, every drop of his blood with Donna.

He moved her up and down with his arms, thrusting into her. She was coming—her moans, louder than ever before, resonated deep in his chest. Her insides began to quiver, milking him, and he held on as long as he could, but finally, he fell over the edge with her.

He came long and hard, giving her every last drop of him and more. She cried and moaned and called his name, and her ecstasy seemed to come in waves for a while.

When he was empty, she fell on top of him and lay panting. They stayed like that for a while, enveloped in each other, breathing in unison, their hearts beating as one.

But then, something broke. He sensed Donna's fear, and she tensed. She slid off of him, a frown on her face, and Sigurd's gut filled with ice.

He did not want to dance around the thing. He had to know. "You are leaving me, aren't you?"

Tears welled in Donna's eyes. "Yes."

"No." The ice spread in his stomach and filled his blood vessels. "Why in Loki's name *now*?"

"I fulfilled my purpose. There is nothing more for me here. No reason to stay."

The ice reached Sigurd's heart. "Nothing?"

The vein in her neck throbbed faster. "Is there?"

"If I asked you to stay"— he swallowed— "would you?"

"I can't, Sigurd."

"Am I not enough a reason?"

He clasped her hand in his, and warmth spread through his skin. Her eyes filled with tears once more.

"Damn it, Sigurd! I knew already last night I needed to leave as soon as possible. I wanted to spend one last night with you, but if I don't leave today— If I don't leave *now*," she said, her voice tapering off to a whisper, "I will never be able to leave you. With every second I spend with you, it's getting harder and harder for me to go."

"Then stay!"

The words hung there like a sail on a mast.

"I can't, Sigurd. My clients... My mother... Our firm... I

won't be able to live with myself if those four women and their children land on the streets because I did not come back."

Sigurd's mouth pressed into a thin line. "Change your mind. That night on the fjord... What we shared then happens only once in a lifetime."

She squeezed his hand gently. "It does. You changed me."

"As did you change me."

Sigurd's chest burned. He was tired of hiding behind the facade of not feeling, of not caring.

If baring his soul couldn't convince her, then nothing would. "You are a treasure for my jarldom. Be my wife, Donna. Be my equal in everything, as I know this is what you desire. You can manage the women, and learn archery, and go on raids with me. What say you?"

Donna listened with an open mouth. She leaned towards him, a broad smile on her face. For a moment, he thought she would say yes, and hope bloomed in his chest.

But Donna brushed the happiness off like water and looked around herself with a concerned expression. "I can't. Where are my clothes? The ones I came here in?"

Panic spread in his blood like liquid iron. He was losing her. "Don't go."

She closed her eyes shut. "Please."

The desire to grab her and lock her under his body in bed and not allow her a step away from him burned in his muscles, and he clenched his fists to keep from throwing himself on her.

"Fine, I'll find them on my own."

One by one, she began opening the chests and rummaging in them. Finally, she found her things and dressed without looking at him. He watched her every move, the play of her muscles under her skin, the swell of her breasts, the curves of her gorgeous backside, her beautiful, thin waist. He wanted to burn the memory of her forever into his soul.

Seeing her dressed in the same strange clothes as when he had first met her made his chest ache. Sigurd put his pants on and took his ax. He gestured her to the door. In the great hall, servants were cleaning after yesterday's victory feast, and they looked up in surprise as Donna walked past them in her own clothes. Her eyes still glistening with tears as she looked around, probably hoping to see Asa.

Outside, people tended to animals, the blacksmith pounded on metal, and the fishermen smoked fish. But the atmosphere was darkened by the preparations for the funeral. People carried firewood and personal belongings of the deceased to the funeral pyre. Floki and many other great warriors had fallen yesterday defending their jarl and their loved ones, and Sigurd prayed to Odin that he would let them all enter Valhöll and that they would wait for him there.

Sigurd's hand clasped Donna's. "I want to touch you every last moment that we have."

Donna squeezed his hand, and Sigurd absorbed the tingling that he always felt when she was close.

When they arrived at the arch, the rocks looked as hard and as unforgiving as before, and there were no traces of any patchwork that glued the fallen rock back to the arch. The palisade smelled of fresh wood and pine tar and looked solid.

Finally, she turned to face him. Tears welled in her eyes. He brought her to him and took her mouth hungrily, desperately. But Donna stopped him.

"I must go. We saved your people, now I need to save mine. You of all people know what duty means."

He rested his forehead against hers. How was it possible that she knew him better than anyone? "I do," he said, breathing out.

She moved to step aside, but his arms kept her in place. Sigurd squeezed her so hard, her bones must have cracked and kissed her with such strength that he almost bit her.

Then he released her and took a step back, and the ground shifted under his feet as if she had just kicked out a supporting beam and he had been left forever off-balance, like a crooked house.

She wiped her tears.

"Goodbye, Sigurd," she whispered. "Treat the women well."

She turned away to walk to the arch, but Sigurd's hand grasped her and whirled her to face him. He removed his Thor's hammer pendant from his neck and gave it to her. Maybe he was giving away his luck, but he would feel better knowing she had some piece of him with her. He hoped it would protect her.

"You are taking my heart with you, Goddess." His warm breath kissed her cheek. "Treat it well, too."

Donna spun and ran towards the gate. It took Sigurd all of his inner strength not to stop her, and then not to take a sledgehammer and smash the arch into dust.

When she reached the gate, she opened it and walked through. Then she turned to him, and he met her eyes for the last time. Eternity connected them, and he thought his heart would explode with love and anguish, a storm-tossed wave against a rock.

And then she was gone.

CHAPTER SEVENTEEN

*D*onna's body ached. She realized she was lying on something cold and hard. She needed to open her eyes, but her eyelids felt like they were stuck together. A fluorescent lamp buzzed somewhere in the distance. The air smelled slightly of bad coffee.

Donna finally opened her eyes, and her heart sank even though she already knew the truth. She was back in New York. She sat upright on the marble floor of the empty courthouse hall. Muffled voices spoke from behind the wooden doors on the left side of the hall. The glass on the fireproof doors at the end of the hall gleamed from the gray daylight falling through the windows.

Sigurd…did he even exist? Had she bumped her head when she fell? Had it all been a dream?

She felt the hard edges of something pressing into the skin of her right palm and opened her hand. A Thor's hammer pendant, warm from her skin, glinted despite the dim light. Sigurd… A giant wound opened in her chest like a black hole. No, he wasn't a dream. Her body felt broken, as if a vital organ had been removed and she now had to live incomplete, half-alive.

Because Sigurd was not in this world.

Donna went home. She probably hailed a cab, although she did not remember. New York overwhelmed her with its honking and shouting.

Donna showered, and warm running water felt like a blessing after bathing in the river for a couple of weeks.

She needed to learn to live without Sigurd now.

Donna had just turned the faucets off when someone banged on her front door. Mother must have heard the water running—she lived in an apartment on the same floor. Donna felt the bite of guilt, put on a bathrobe, and rushed to open the door.

Mother, her eyes wide, hugged her tight, as the familiar scent of Chanel No.5 enveloped Donna.

"I thought I lost you," Mom whispered into Donna's wet hair. "Where the hell have you been?"

Donna closed her eyes, and tears ran down her face. "I traveled back in time."

Her mother gave a laugh, pushed her out of the hug and studied her from the length of her straightened arms.

"Are you all right?"

"I'm fine, Mom." Donna let her mom in and they went to the living room.

"Did you go on a soul-searching trip or something because of Daniel?"

"Something like that."

"This is so not like you. But I understand. After Joseph, I had to gather my life in pieces, too. But why didn't you call me? How could you just abandon your case? I had to manage the firm on my own. The police finally started to search for you. You were gone nine days!"

Donna's eyebrows rose. After all the crazy stuff she had

been through, she should have not been surprised that time could run at different speeds. She'd spent two and a half weeks with Sigurd, and yet here only nine days had passed. "I'm sorry, Mom. I'll call them and explain. How is the case?"

"I managed to pause things, but you know the clients need us to win."

"We will." Although Donna said that, she did not feel like a warrior-lawyer at all. All she wanted to do was find the Norn and go back to Sigurd. But she could not leave those four single mothers in poverty.

"When is the next hearing?"

"In a week."

Donna rubbed her face with her palms. All she felt was exhaustion.

"Seriously, where have you been?" Mom regarded her closely now.

If Donna told her the truth, repeated what she'd said about time traveling in a serious manner, her mother would take her to a psycho ward. "It's like you said. I needed some time off. I was in Vermont."

"But you could have sent an email. A text… Something."

"I met a man, and he turned my world upside down." Oh, it felt good to tell this to someone. "And I needed to help him with something, but I lost the track of time."

"Who is he?"

"He's from far away, and I'll never see him again."

Tears sprung from her eyes as a wound the size of a basketball opened up and started to bleed inside her chest. Mom hugged her and soothed her the best she could.

"Oh, honey, we should stay away from men. I raised you to be independent. This is what they can do to you. Break your heart, destroy your spirit—"

Donna sat upright. Before Sigurd, she would have agreed. Now, she felt that her mother could not be more wrong.

"Stop." She remembered what Sigurd had told her. "Some people plant rotten seeds in us, and we let them. I love him. He's driven, and commanding, and stubborn. But he is also the kindest, strongest man in the world."

And he is a Viking jarl, she wanted to add, but she kept her mouth shut.

"He changed me, Mom. I don't think that all men are bad. Or all alpha-males. It's just that they, too, have their own pain. Everyone does."

Mother frowned. "Honey, you seem different."

She raised her chin. "And I am not afraid of them anymore."

She went back to work the very next day and plunged back into the case so that she'd forget him. She had hoped it would get easier with the time, but it only got harder. Her anguish over Sigurd intensified with each day. The only thing that kept her going was the need to help her clients.

A week passed, and the pain of losing Sigurd grew like an ulcer. After a month, Donna barely recognized herself. Whenever she found herself alone or having a quiet second, the feeling of loss drenched her like a downpour.

* * *

WHILE DONNA WORKED hard on the case, Marta's baby, Juan, arrived, and Helena's girl, Eloisa, followed. And despite the hardships, the babies were bathed in love and did not need a thing thanks to a small community in one part of Bronx that reminded Donna of the spirit of Vörnen.

With two new little people to protect, Donna tripled her efforts. She could not allow herself to lose. She had too much on the line. She had sacrificed too much to be here.

The final hearing came three months after Donna returned to New York. Daniel met her in the courthouse waiting room with his usual smug smile. He looked her up and down. Before, it would have set her cheeks on fire. Now, it seemed funny.

In the courtroom, he did everything to intimidate her, to push her emotional buttons. But Donna did not care. Something had changed in her. It was as if Sigurd were with her, giving her inner strength, igniting the Viking spirit in her. Her clients watched her with wide, hope-filled eyes.

The manager of the Cinederellas Inc., Pedro Ferreira—the one who had fired the ladies—was called to the witness stand, and after some questioning, Donna knew she was close.

"Why were my clients fired, Mr. Ferreira?"

"Because they did not do their job well."

"And why was that?"

"They became slow and lazy."

Triumph spread through Donna. "They *became* slow and lazy?"

Mr. Ferreira paled. Daniel jumped up but only opened and closed his mouth.

"All four of them?"

He kept silent.

Donna brought a few papers to Daniel and to the judge. "Your Honor, these are the records from my clients' doctors. During their pregnancies, Ms. Hernández had high blood pressure. Ms. Garcia had a case of hyperemesis gravidarum —which means excessive vomiting. And Ms. Gonzalez and Ms. Ramos luckily had healthy pregnancies but still were more tired than before, which is a normal pregnancy symptom. So, I can see how their condition would make them slower when they cleaned houses. The dates of the medical records are all within weeks of the date they were fired."

"Permission to approach the bench, Your Honor?" Daniel said.

The judge nodded, and Donna and Daniel both came to him.

Daniel's eyes were angry behind the facade of calmness. He'd lost, and all three knew that. "I'd like to invite the opposing council to discuss settlement."

A good settlement was exactly what Donna and her clients wanted. In the negotiation room, Daniel started with one hundred thousand dollars, but Donna got him up to half a million. She eyed him in triumph, her hand playing with the Sigurd's Thor hammer pendant as if she could somehow touch Sigurd through it.

She said, "Five hundred thousand, and let your client publicly apologize to them and implement a non-discrimination policy in the workplace. I want Mr. Ferreira to attend and then teach non-discrimination workshops at Cinderellas Inc."

Daniel rolled his eyes but stretched his hand out for a shake. "I'll talk to my client."

When the deal was signed an hour later, triumph exploded in Donna like fireworks. She'd won! The ladies could now start new lives without worrying if they would be able to feed their children tomorrow. She touched Sigurd's pendant again, and anguish filled her.

What she wanted now, more than anything in the whole world, was to share this victory with the one person she could not. The man she loved more than anything in this world.

Sigurd.

Donna felt as if she was sinking. Would this be her life from now on? Every time she succeeded, or failed, or anything significant happened in her life, she'd want to share it with Sigurd. She'd fulfilled her obligation to her clients. Was there anything else holding her here?

Mother.

Donna loved her mom, but she could not sacrifice her happiness for her mother. She needed to live her life, and although she'd miss her mom, surely she'd understand.

But Mom needed help with the firm. How could Donna just leave her to manage things alone?

Donna glanced up as Daniel passed by her on his way to the door. Sigurd had changed. Perhaps she owed Daniel that opportunity, as well.

"Daniel, I am leaving New York," she called out, "and I want to offer you my partnership."

He turned and stared at her, his eyes wide. "What?"

When they used to be close, Daniel had told her he'd love to build his own firm from the ground up. She needed to make him see that was what she was offering.

After a long conversation, Donna got him thinking.

Daniel said, "You are just a two-woman show, right? You and your mother?"

"Right. But we have more cases than we can handle. New York will never run out of discrimination suits, and we are building a name for ourselves. But if a lawyer with hunger and ambition joined, combined with my mother's experience, the firm would become legendary." She tapped a finger on her lip. "If only there was such a person…"

Daniel laughed. "I know what you are doing."

"Yeah. You do. But how do you think your father would feel if your firm beat the giants he had expected you to work for? Would he respect you even more?"

Daniel lowered his gaze and said his next words in a pained whisper. "I never intended to offend you or any other woman. When you accused me of taking Marta's seat, it was like a kick in my face. I never wanted to become this. This attitude towards women, it's like— It's as if it's part of the job description."

Donna smiled. "So quit the job."

CHAPTER EIGHTEEN

*D*onna's heart squeezed in anticipation as she saw the end of the fjord approaching with colorful Scandinavian houses scattered on the hills.

Vörnen.

There was no wooden fortress, no longhouses, and no dragonships. But the same tall walls of the mountains, the pebbled beach, and the gray autumn undergrowth where Sigurd and she had made love stole her breath away.

The boat docked and the tourists walked off. Donna waited until everyone else had descended. Then she savored the moment when her feet touched the ground where every pebble and grain of sand was soaked in Sigurd's presence.

It was just the day before yesterday that had Donna won the case, and the urge to find Sigurd had become more powerful than the need to breath. Donna worried if Sigurd had forgotten all about her, since who knew how much time had passed back in his time. Had he gotten married? Did he have any children by now? The thought made her skin clammy and made her chest clench till it ached.

On the bright side, Daniel had quickly agreed to become

a partner in the firm. Mother was having a hard time accepting the idea, even after his offer of a very impressive buy-in.

Donna's conscience was clean. Donna had told her that she'd likely never return and wouldn't be able to have contact with her for reasons beyond her control. But that she'd be very happy with the man she loved. The morning Donna had to leave, Mom had driven her to the airport but hadn't wanted to go inside.

She'd kept silent for a while, then looked at Donna with bloodshot eyes. "You are brave, Donna. You are doing something I wouldn't have dared to do—not after Joseph."

Donna squeezed her hand. "Thank you, Mom. I love you." She hugged her and walked out of the car with a sunken heart. Mom rolled the window down and said, "I'll be brave, too. I'll accept Daniel."

The air in Vörnen did not taste as sweet as she remembered, Donna thought as she rolled a tiny carry-on over the icy pavement. She wore the most practical clothes she could think of: jeans, a thick sweater, and the warmest and most durable boots she could find. Her carry-on contained medicine, underwear, warm clothes, a few hygienic items, and books. She'd miss books.

Even though Donna would miss her mother, she felt at peace with her. She felt like she'd said her goodbye.

Donna did not even book a lodging in Vörnen. With sweating palms and a pounding heart, she walked straight to the arch, almost not recognizing which way to go. Was she in the right place? It was as if this was not Vörnen at all. No chickens, no goats, no men with axes nor women in apron dresses. Instead, the rustle of passing cars against the asphalt, the smell of vanilla from a bakery, stern faces of people leaving a bank. This all seemed too normal, too real, as if Sigurd, the fortress, and his people had never even existed.

She swallowed a hard knot. But they had, they must have. Her heavy boots thumped against the asphalt faster and faster, until she was running towards the west where she saw the forest behind the roofs of the houses. This must be where the arch had been.

Donna's pulse pounded in her temples as the last dark-red house of the village revealed two rock walls and a foot-worn pathway. No palisade.

And no arch.

Donna dropped the handle of her carry-on and ran towards the rocks, her feet heavy.

No, no, no. This could not be.

Her hands were glued to the rock wall, hungry to feel that sensation of being sucked in, but nothing happened. Magic did not fill the cold, rough surface. They were just rocks.

Life must have left her for a moment. Her heart skipped a beat, her mind went blank, and despair poured over her like a bucket of ice water.

She hit the rocks with both palms. "Take me back, damn you!" The sharp parts stabbed her skin, but the pain did not matter. She slid down the rock and just sat there. The sun began to descend and she blinked as its gentle light tickled her eyes through the bare branches of the trees.

This was it. No more Sigurd. This time, for real.

Donna stood up from the ground and could barely straighten her back. Her stomach hurt as if there was a ragged wound in the center of her body.

Tears burned her eyes and she did not stop them. What would she do now? Was there any coming back from this? Was it even worth living this life, a life without Sigurd?

Donna walked towards her carry-on where it lay by the path. She picked it up and rolled it down the path towards the village. She probably needed to find somewhere to stay for tonight, not that she cared if she slept under a bridge or in a bed.

As she passed by a few houses, a glint of gold somewhere to the side caught her eye, and she glanced there. On top of a house with a low, thatched roof sat an old woman. She was knitting and waved her hand at Donna. Needles prickled Donna's skin when she recognized the Norn.

Donna hurried to the building, and the Norn began speaking a foreign language that sounded oddly familiar. Seeing that Donna did not understand her, the woman switched to English, "Oh, I forgot you don't speak Old Norse in this century. I wanted to say I was surprised when you left Sigurd."

The golden spindle lay next to the woman, and Donna's mouth became as dry as sandpaper.

"Send me back." Hope started to fill Donna, but she forbade it to. It was too early to hope. Her palms were covered in sweat.

The Norn smiled at her like a good old universal grandma. "Your tapestry shone when you were back there, with Sigurd."

"Will you send me then?"

"If I do, you won't be able to come back. You won't get any more chances."

Donna's throat clenched. "I am ready."

The Norn jumped off the roof like a little girl. With a soft smile, she held out the golden spindle.

"Don't forget your luggage." She winked at Donna.

Donna grabbed the handle of her carry-on and took a deep breath. "Sigurd, I'm coming," she thought and took the spindle. The Norn and the Scandinavian houses disappeared. Pain wracked Donna as she felt as if the blood was sucked out of her, and she began spinning like the golden spindle.

* * *

SIGURD WAS on his way back from hunting, a deer carcass thrown over his shoulders. There was not much to do in winter other than hunt, fish, drink and tell stories that made the gods, the Norns, and the giants come alive. Winter was full of songs that people sang together in the smoky air of longhouses, firepits that glowed in the darkness of the long nights, and the crunch of snow as you walked from house to house in search of a new story or a fresh pint of mead.

The western gate darkened in twilight in front of him. Whenever he had to pass through it, he flinched, the ghost of Donna ever present. It tortured him. He avoided looking at it and chased away the hope of seeing her. Desperation clawed at his heart like a hungry lynx.

Once, he had even gone to the arch intending to find the way to time travel to the future, to Donna.

But nothing had happened.

And nothing would. He'd just need to learn to live with the pain.

He opened the gate to walk towards the village and saw a figure standing with her back to him. She was dressed in strange clothes, had long golden hair, and was the same height and build as his goddess. His heart froze, as if afraid to make the next beat.

She turned in that moment, and time stood still.

Donna.

Their eyes locked. Sigurd took a step towards her but fell to his knees, the deer carcass dropping to the snow next to him. She glowed as if the stars from the sky had descended and filled her whole body with their light. Did his mind just show him what he had been imagining for so long?

"Is that you?" A cloud of condensation from his mouth brought the words out in a gasp.

Donna rushed to him, her cheeks pink from the frost, her hair falling in a golden cascade. She fell to her knees right in front of him and took his gloved hands in hers.

"I came back."

He removed his suede gloves and grasped her hands again to check if he could really feel them, and they burned his skin with their coolness. She must have been outside for some time.

Donna reached out to kiss him, but he leaned back. Before he could believe she really was here, he had to know. "Why?" he searched her face for signs of the answer he craved to hear.

"Because I love you." Donna's eyes glimmered like the sea under the summer sun.

If Thor had struck him with lightning, he would not be more affected. A ringing vibration went through his body as if he were a string on a lyre. Tears burned the corners of his eyes.

"As do I—with everything that I am, my Goddess."

He kissed her, the taste of her so familiar and so sweet, the scent of her making the world spin as if he had just drunk mead the likes of which was only served by Odin in Valhöll.

"I'll break the arch tomorrow," he growled into her mouth. "You are stuck with me forever."

"Promise?"

"Swear to all gods."

EPILOGUE

 örnen, 872 AD

SIGURD STOOD on the pier hugging Donna with one arm, Vigdis in front of him. Waves splashed against the hull of the ship that rocked next to the dock behind his sister. A steady breeze filled the sail—the longship was ready to set off. It looked like Njord, god of the sea and the winds, favored Vigdis's journey.

His goddess looked radiant and healthy with her swollen belly. They were not yet married because Sigurd wanted to make a legendary feast out of their wedding and celebrate it at the harvest festival. He'd invited all neighboring jarls and kings to strengthen their relationships and start new trading alliances. He had learned too painfully the price of clinging to rivalry.

The fortress stood whole and strong. The women had helped to finish it last year, after Donna had left. But ever since she'd gotten back in the winter, she'd managed to involve them more and more, and the village had begun to thrive like never before. The women weaved sails, hunted, and fished. Through winter, they crafted furniture, learned to make jewelry, and carved breathtaking patterns on wood. Some of those who'd constructed the fortress helped build new ships, and the frames of three longships grew daily by the fjord.

The news of Vörnen's strength and of Sigurd's victory traveled fast, and new warriors came looking to serve a strong jarl. He'd go raiding in a couple of weeks to finally replenish the treasury and be able to sustain the loyalty of his warriors. Nothing would have been possible without Donna and without the women of his jarldom.

The ship rocked gently next to the dock.

"There should be enough silver to buy you a rich farm in Iceland," Sigurd said.

Vigdis nodded. Sacks with provisions and sea chests with food, clothes, tools, and enough silver for her new life stood there. Bjarni Bjarnison, the man who had brought the message of Fuldarr's attack, waited for Vigdis on the boat together with a dozen warriors that Sigurd had given to his sister for protection and for rowing. Vigdis glanced back at the beach.

"This is where it all began." Pain flickered through her face. "Where he died."

Sigurd shook his head. "It began much earlier than that. But will it end now?"

"Now that I have seen the consequences of what I did, I don't want to be a jarl. All I ever wanted was to have some power over my own life and some influence in our house. Father never gave me the chance to do that, and the desire grew like a rot-wound. I thought I wanted to be part of the world of kings and jarls. But this"—she circled the beach with her hand—"I want none of it. A farm, a good husband"—she glanced back at Bjarni and blushed—"and a child." She gave a warm smile to Donna. "That would be enough. I'll have plenty of things to manage. Fuldarr's jarldom is yours, brother. After his warriors saw you in the battle, they know they won't find a stronger jarl. So you won't have any resistance once you visit the lands."

"Do I have your word that you won't decide to reclaim the jarldom?"

"I swear, brother," she said in a suppressed whisper, as if a beast slept nearby and she'd wake it up if she spoke any louder.

"Good."

She hugged him, and the scent of her touched his face for a moment, reminding him of their mother, and his heart squeezed. Vigdis brushed off her tears, turned to the boat, and Bjarni helped her get in. As the men pushed the boat away from the dock with the oars, Donna said, "You'll come to the wedding, won't you? Both of you?"

Vigdis's face brightened. "The journey should take us a couple of weeks. In three months, we should be settled. We'll come."

Sigurd nodded. He was looking forward to the abundance of the harvest festival: tables full of fresh vegetables, roasted boars, hares, and deer, smoked salmon, and new mead. The feeling of home and family. His family.

"Goodbye!" Vigdis called as the boat moved further into the distance.

A feeling of peace spread through Sigurd like a cool wave on a warm day. Bjarni laid his arm on Vigdis's shoulder in the same manner that Sigurd's arm was on Donna's. They waved to Sigurd and Donna.

"Do you believe her word?" Donna asked.

Sigurd squinted against the reflection of the sun on the fjord's surface, following the ship with his eyes. "I do."

"Why?"

"She's changed. Not only because she saw the results of her betrayal. But because of love. I can see that as clearly as I see you. Bjarni changed her." He kissed Donna gently, and his body started simmering with desire. "Just like you changed me. I can even understand why she took our enemy's side. Every person needs to feel valued and useful, and she did not have that. But I hope you do. I am grateful to have such strong women in my jarldom and especially at my side."

Donna smiled and laid her head on his shoulder. "I could never have dreamed I'd have such a strong man by my side."

The boat disappeared behind a mountain, and Sigurd and Donna walked back home. The feeling of peace spread from his chest further into his body. As they approached the fortress, Sigurd stopped Donna by the open gate. As he glanced at the fortress that had brought her here, a feeling of wholeness spread through him, repairing the remains of the wounds in his soul like a healing balm.

He knelt before Donna and laid his palms on her swollen belly. His fingers felt a small kick, and he planted a kiss on the spot. He looked up at Donna from where he knelt, overwhelmed by the love that grew in every muscle of his body and that he saw reflected in her eyes.

"The Norn is weaving a beautiful tapestry from my life," he said. "Because it's everything I could ever wish for. You, the child," Donna's fingers brushed through his hair, and his scalp tingled, "and something we built together. The fortress of time."

A glimpse into
    THE JEWEL OF TIME

CHICAGO, 2018

THE NORN SMILED AS, out of the corner of her eye, she saw a young woman's hand stretching out to grasp the spindle. The three Norns were having lunch on a bench at Navy Pier, enjoying the view of Lake Michigan and the sun's rays warming their ancient skin. The woman thought the Norn did not see what she was up to. She needed to gather money fast for her mother's kidney transplant, and stealth seemed to be her only remaining choice.

But she had no idea that on the other side of that spindle, a young Viking needed her more than air to breathe.

As her fingers touched the golden surface, the woman disappeared, and the Norn began knitting, enjoying the story unfolding in the scarf.

TO BE the first to be notified of the book release, sign up at mariahstone.com/jewel-launch/.

JOIN THE ROMANCE TIME-TRAVELERS' CLUB!

Join the mailing list on mariahstone.com to receive exclusive bonuses, author insights, release announcements, giveaways and the insider scoop of books on sale—and more!

Upcoming books in the series:

One Night with a Viking

The Jewel of Time

The Marriage of Time

The Surf of Time

The Tree of Time

ENJOY THE BOOK? YOU CAN MAKE A DIFFERENCE!

Please, leave your honest review!

As much as I'd love to, I don't have financial capacity like New York publishers to run ads in the newspaper or put posters in subway.
But I have something much, much more powerful!

Committed and loyal readers

If you enjoyed the book, I'd be so grateful if you could spend five minutes leaving a review on the book's Amazon page.

Thank you very much!

WITHOUT YOU, THE BOOK WOULD
NOT HAVE BEEN POSSIBLE...

...**my husband** and **my son,** the loves of my life, for whom I do this.

...**my parents** and **my sister** who support me in every step.

...the best romance editor in the world **Laura Barth** who has superpowers.

...my mentor, **Michael Marano**, who taught me about writing smart commercial fiction.

...**Mark Dawson**, **James Blatch** and the whole **SPF community** without whom I'd still be dreaming about being published.

...**Bryan Cohen** who wrote the amazing book description that makes The Fortress shine.

...**Annette Maxberry-Carrara and the Düsseldorf writing group** who gave me back my belief in myself as a writer.

...**AJ Silvers** who opened my eyes to the reality of being indie published.

...my writer friends, **Nicky Hugill, Joe L. Murr, Linn Steenhoek, Astird Buchard, Javier Gonzalez, Elena de**

Francisco, Sofia Borgstein, Tadhg Scullyand all members of my local writing group. Every second Saturday in our library is a highlight.

...my readers who make it all possible.

Mariah xxx

ABOUT MARIAH STONE

Mariah Stone fell in love with her future husband on the edge of a Norwegian fjord. Now she lives in the Netherlands with him and their baby son. Her talents include forgetting everything when she writes and creating a bigger mess than her baby can ever make.

She believes love wins even if people come from different backgrounds – even if they were born hundreds of years apart.

That's what her books are about.

Manufactured by Amazon.ca
Bolton, ON